PENGUIN CLASSICS
*Maigret's First Case*

'I love reading Simenon. He makes me think of Chekhov'
– William Faulkner

'A truly wonderful writer . . . marvellously readable – lucid, simple, absolutely in tune with the world he creates'
– Muriel Spark

'Few writers have ever conveyed with such a sure touch, the bleakness of human life'　　　　– A. N. Wilson

'One of the greatest writers of the twentieth century . . . Simenon was unequalled at making us look inside, though the ability was masked by his brilliance at absorbing us obsessively in his stories'　　　　– *Guardian*

'A novelist who entered his fictional world as if he were part of it'　　　　– Peter Ackroyd

'The greatest of all, the most genuine novelist we have had in literature'　　　　– André Gide

'Superb . . . The most addictive of writers . . . A unique teller of tales'　　　　– *Observer*

'The mysteries of the human personality are revealed in all their disconcerting complexity'　　　　– Anita Brookner

'A writer who, more than any other crime novelist, combined a high literary reputation with popular appeal'　　– P. D. James

'A supreme writer . . . Unforgettable vividness' – *Independent*

'Compelling, remorseless, brilliant'　　　　– John Gray

'Extraordinary masterpieces of the twentieth century'
– John Banville

## ABOUT THE AUTHOR

Georges Simenon was born on 12 February 1903 in Liège, Belgium, and died in 1989 in Lausanne, Switzerland, where he had lived for the latter part of his life. Between 1931 and 1972 he published seventy-five novels and twenty-eight short stories featuring Inspector Maigret.

Simenon always resisted identifying himself with his famous literary character, but acknowledged that they shared an important characteristic:

> My motto, to the extent that I have one, has been noted often enough, and I've always conformed to it. It's the one I've given to old Maigret, who resembles me in certain points . . . 'understand and judge not'.

Penguin is publishing the entire series of Maigret novels.

# GEORGES SIMENON

# Maigret's First Case

*Translated by* ROS SCHWARTZ

PENGUIN BOOKS

PENGUIN CLASSICS

UK | USA | Canada | Ireland | Australia
India | New Zealand | South Africa

Penguin Books is part of the Penguin Random House group of companies
whose addresses can be found at global.penguinrandomhouse.com.

 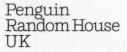

First published, in instalments, in *Point de vue / Images du monde* between 24 February and 30 June 1949
First published in book form as *La première enquête de Maigret* by Presses de la Cité 1949
This translation first published 2016
002

Set in Dante MT Std 12.5/15pt
Typeset by Palimpsest Book Production Limited, Falkirk, Stirlingshire
Printed in Great Britain by Clays Ltd, St Ives plc

ISBN: 978–0–241–20638–6

www.greenpenguin.co.uk

# Contents

# 1. The Flautist's Statement

The room was divided in two by a black railing. In the section reserved for the public, there was only one bench, also painted black, against the whitewashed wall plastered with official notices. On the other side were desks, inkstands and pigeonholes bulging with fat black files, so that everything was black and white. Standing on a metal base was a cast-iron stove of the kind now only found in provincial railway stations, with a flue that rose up to the ceiling and then formed an elbow to cross the entire room before disappearing into the wall.

A chubby-faced officer called Lecœur had unbuttoned his uniform and was trying to sleep.

The hands on the black-rimmed clock showed 1.25. Every now and then, the single gas lamp would sputter. Every now and then too, the stove, for no apparent reason, would begin to hum.

Outside, the quiet of the night was disturbed occasionally by the sound of firecrackers at growing intervals, the singing of a drunkard or a cab clattering down the sloping street.

Sitting at the desk on the left, the secretary of the Saint-Georges district police station, his lips moving silently like a schoolboy, was poring over a newly published little manual: *Guide to Official Reports (Verbal Descriptions) for the Use of Police Officers and Inspectors.*

On the flyleaf, handwritten in capital letters in purple ink was the name: J. Maigret.

Three times already that night the young police secretary had got up to go over and poke the stove, and for the rest of his life he would feel nostalgic for that particular stove. It was identical, or almost, to the one he would find one day at Quai des Orfèvres and later on, when central heating was installed at the headquarters of the Police Judiciaire, Detective Chief Inspector Maigret, head of the Crime Squad, would manage to keep that stove in his office.

This was 15 April 1913. In those days, the Police Judiciaire was still called the Sûreté. That morning, a foreign head of state had arrived at Longchamp station amid great pomp, and the President had been there to welcome him. The official carriages, flanked by the Republican Guard in full dress uniform, had marched down Avenue du Bois and along the Champs-Élysées lined with flags and people.

There had been a gala performance at the Opéra, fireworks and parades, and only now was the noise of the boisterous crowds beginning to die down.

The police were overwhelmed. Despite all the precautions taken, the preventive arrests, the deals made with certain reputedly dangerous individuals, there had been fears of an anarchist bomb up until the last minute.

Maigret and Lecœur were alone, at 1.30 in the morning, at the Saint-Georges district police station in the quiet Rue La-Rochefoucauld.

They both looked up on hearing hurried footsteps outside. The door opened. A breathless young man stood glancing about him, dazzled by the gas light.

'The chief inspector?' he panted.

'I'm his secretary,' said Maigret without getting up.

He didn't yet know that this was the start of his first case.

The man was fair-haired and slight, with blue eyes and a pink complexion. He wore a beige coat over his black suit and was holding a bowler hat, while his other hand kept gingerly touching his swollen nose.

'Were you attacked by some ruffian?'

'No. I was trying to go to the assistance of a woman who was shouting for help.'

'In the street?'

'No, in a big house in Rue Chaptal. I think you'd better come right away. They threw me out.'

'Who?'

'A sort of butler or concierge.'

'Don't you think you'd better begin at the beginning? What were you doing in Rue Chaptal?'

'I was on my way home from work. My name is Justin Minard. I am second flautist at the Concerts Lamoureux, but at night I play at the Brasserie Clichy, Boulevard de Clichy. I live in Rue d'Enghien, just opposite the Petit Parisien. As usual, I walked down Rue Ballu, then Rue Chaptal.'

Ever the conscientious secretary, Maigret took notes.

'About halfway down the street, which is nearly always empty, I noticed a parked motor-car, a De Dion-Bouton, with its engine running. At the wheel there was a man wearing a grey goatskin jacket, his face almost entirely hidden behind enormous goggles. As I drew level with him, a second-floor window opened.'

'Did you take note of the house number?'

'Seventeen A. It's a private mansion with a carriage entrance. There were no lights in any other windows. Only the second from the left, the one that opened. I looked up and saw the shape of a woman trying to lean out, and she shouted: "Help!"'

'What did you do?'

'Wait. Someone in the room must have dragged her away from the window. At the same time, a shot rang out. I turned round to look at the car I'd just passed, and it sped off.'

'Are you certain it wasn't the sound of the engine back-firing that you heard?'

'Absolutely positive. I went up to the door and rang the bell.'

'Were you alone?'

'Yes.'

'Armed?'

'No.'

'What did you intend to do?'

'Well . . .'

The flautist was so thrown by the question that he was stumped for a reply. Had it not been for his blond moustache and a few wisps on his chin, he would have looked barely more than sixteen.

'Didn't the neighbours hear anything?'

'Apparently not.'

'Did they open up the door to you?'

'Not right away. I rang at least three times. Then I started kicking the door. Eventually I heard footsteps, then a chain being removed and a bolt pulled back. There was no light in the porch, but there's a gas lamp just outside the house.'

One forty-seven. From time to time the flautist glanced anxiously at the clock.

'A tall fellow in a butler's black suit asked what I wanted.'

'Was he fully dressed?'

'Of course.'

'With his trousers and tie?'

'Yes.'

'And yet there were no lights on in the house?'

'Except in the second-floor bedroom.'

'What did you say?'

'I don't know. I tried to get inside.'

'Why?'

'To go and see for myself. He barred my path. I told him about the woman who'd shouted from the window.'

'Did he seem flustered?'

'He glared at me and pushed me away with all his weight.'

'Then what?'

'He muttered that I'd been imagining things, that I was drunk and things like that. Then there was a voice in the darkness. It sounded as if it was coming from the first-floor landing.'

'What did the voice say?'

'"Hurry up, Louis!"'

'Then what?'

'He gave me a violent shove and when I resisted, he

punched me in the face. I ended up sprawled on the ground in front of the closed door.'

'Was the second-floor light still on?'

'No.'

'Did the car come back?'

'No. Hadn't we better go there right away?'

'We? Are you planning to come with me?'

It was both comic and touching, the contrast between the flautist's almost feminine delicateness and his determined air.

'I'm the one who was punched in the face, aren't I? At any rate, I'm going to make a complaint.'

'As you have every right to do.'

'But it would be better if we left that till later, don't you think?'

'Did you tell me the number of the house?'

'Seventeen A.'

Maigret frowned, as that address vaguely rang a bell. He pulled one of the files from its pigeonhole, leafed through it and read a name that made him frown even harder.

He was wearing a tailcoat that night, his first ever tailcoat. A memo had been sent round a few days earlier instructing all police auxiliaries to wear ceremonial dress for the duration of the royal visit, since any one of them could be summoned to join the dignitaries at any moment.

His beige overcoat, bought off the peg, was identical to Justin Minard's.

'Come on! Lecœur, if anyone asks for me, tell them I'll be back soon.'

He was slightly intimidated. The name he had just read in the register did not exactly put him at ease.

He was twenty-six and had been married just five months. Since he had joined the police, four years earlier, he had worked in the lowliest departments — street duty, railway stations, department stores — and he had been secretary at the Saint-Georges district police station for less than a year.

Now the most distinguished name in the entire neighbourhood was that of the inhabitants of 17A Rue Chaptal.

Gendreau-Balthazar. Balthazar Coffee. That name ran in big brown letters along the corridors of the Métro, while in the streets the Balthazar vans, drawn by four magnificent horses, were part of the Paris landscape.

Maigret drank Balthazar coffee. And whenever he walked along Avenue de l'Opéra, on reaching a certain point next to a gunsmith's, he never failed to stop to inhale the delicious smell of coffee being roasted in the window of the Balthazar shop.

The night was cold and clear. There wasn't a soul in the steep street, not a cab in the vicinity. In those days, Maigret was almost as thin as the flautist, so skinny that as they walked up the road they looked like two raw-boned adolescents.

'I presume you haven't been drinking?'

'I never drink. Doctor's orders.'

'Are you certain you saw a window opening?'

'I'm absolutely positive.'

This was the first time that Maigret was standing on his own two feet. Until now he had merely accompanied his boss, Monsieur Le Bret, the most urbane detective chief inspector in Paris, on various raids, four of them to establish proof of adultery.

Rue Chaptal was as deserted as Rue La-Rochefoucauld. There were no lights on in the Gendreau-Balthazar residence, one of the finest mansions in the neighbourhood.

'You said that there was a parked motor-car?'

'Yes, right here.'

Not quite outside the door. A little higher up the street. Maigret, whose head was buzzing with fresh theories about Minard's testimony, lit a candle-match and bent over to examine the wood-block paving.

'You see!' exclaimed the musician, triumphantly pointing to a large puddle of blackish oil.

'Come on. I think it's highly irregular for you to be with me.'

'But I'm the one who got punched in the face!'

The situation was actually rather alarming. As he raised his hand to ring the bell, Maigret felt his chest tighten, and he wondered which regulation he could invoke. He had no warrant. Besides, it was the middle of the night. Could he really claim a crime had been committed when his only evidence was the flautist's swollen nose?

Like the musician, he had to ring three times, but he did not have to kick the door. At length a voice called out:

'What is it?'

'Police!' he said in a slightly tremulous voice.

'One moment, please. I'll get the key.'

There was a click inside the porch. The house already had electricity. Then they had to wait for ages.

'It's him,' said the musician, who had recognized the voice.

At last, the chain was removed and the bolt drawn back to reveal a sleepy face with eyes that slid over Maigret and stared at Justin Minard.

'Ah! You've caught him!' said the man. 'I suppose he tried his little prank on you?'

'May we come in?'

'If you must. Please keep quiet so as not to wake the entire household. Come this way.'

To the left, up three marble steps, was a glazed double door that led to a colonnaded hall. It was the first time that Maigret had ever been inside such an opulent residence, whose proportions reminded him of the splendour of a ministerial building.

'Is your name Louis?'

'How do you know?'

All the same, Louis opened a door that led not into the drawing room, but into a sort of butler's pantry. He looked as if he had just got out of bed as he wasn't wearing his livery but a white nightshirt with a red-embroidered collar and a hastily pulled-on pair of trousers.

'Is Monsieur Gendreau-Balthazar at home?'

'Which one, the father or the son?'

'The father.'

'Monsieur Félicien has not come home yet, and Monsieur Richard, the son, probably retired hours ago. Now, about half an hour ago, this drunkard . . .'

Louis was tall and burly. He must have been around forty-five, his shaved chin had a five o'clock shadow, his eyes were very dark, his eyebrows black and unusually bushy.

With the feeling that he was jumping in at the deep end, Maigret took a big breath and said:

'I should like to speak to Monsieur Richard.'

'Do you want me to wake him up?'

'Yes please.'

'Would you show me your police ID?'

Maigret held out his Préfecture card.

'Have you been in this neighbourhood long?'

'Ten months.'

'And you are based at Saint-Georges?'

'That's right.'

'Then you must know Monsieur Le Bret?'

'He's my boss.'

Then Louis said, with a casual air that barely concealed a threat:

'I know him too. I have the honour of waiting on him each time he comes here to lunch or dinner.'

He let a few seconds tick by, his gaze elsewhere.

'Do you still want me to wake Monsieur Richard?'

'Yes.'

'Do you have a warrant?'

'No.'

'Very good. Please wait here.'

Before leaving the room, he took from a cupboard a starched shirt-front, a collar and a black tie. Then he put on his morning coat which was hanging up.

There was only one chair in the butler's pantry. Neither Maigret nor Justin Minard sat down. They were enveloped by silence. The entire house was in semi-darkness. It was all very solemn, very daunting.

Twice, Maigret took out his fob watch. Twenty minutes went by before Louis reappeared, still as frosty.

'If you would be so good as to step this way . . .'

Minard attempted to follow Maigret, but the butler turned to him.

'Not you. Unless you are also a police officer.'

Maigret had a ridiculous thought. It seemed cowardly to leave the pallid flautist behind. The butler's pantry with dark wood panelling fleetingly made him think of a sort of dungeon, and he had a vision of the butler with his stubble-covered chin coming back to beat up his victim.

He followed Louis across the colonnaded hall and up the red-carpeted stairs.

A few solitary lamps with yellowish filaments gave out a wan glow, leaving vast areas of darkness. A door on to the first-floor landing was open. A man in a dressing gown stood framed in the light.

'I understand you wish to speak to me? Do come in. That will be all, Louis.'

The room was a sitting room-cum-study with leather-covered walls. A smell of Havana cigar and a fragrance that Maigret could not identify hung in the air. A half-open door led into a bedroom where there was a rumpled four-poster bed.

Richard Gendreau-Balthazar was wearing pyjamas beneath his dressing gown, and on his feet were Russian leather slippers.

He appeared to be around thirty years old. He was

dark-haired and his face would have been quite ordinary were it not for his crooked nose.

'Louis tells me you are from the local police station?'

He opened a carved cigarette box and pushed it towards his visitor, who refused.

'You don't smoke?'

'Only a pipe.'

'I shan't invite you to smoke in here as I can't stand the smell of pipe tobacco. I presume you telephoned my friend Le Bret before coming here?'

'No.'

'Ah! Forgive me if I'm not familiar with the ways of the police. Le Bret is a regular visitor to our house — not, I must emphasize, in a professional capacity. One would never guess he's a police chief! He really is a very charming man and his wife is delightful. Now, let's get to the point. What time is it?'

He made a show of looking for his watch, and it was Maigret who pulled his fat silver turnip watch out of his pocket.

'Twenty-five past two.'

'And it gets light at around five o'clock at this time of year, doesn't it? I know because I often go riding in the Bois de Boulogne very early. I thought that during the hours between sunset and sunrise a citizen's privacy was sacrosanct.'

'That is correct, but—'

He interrupted Maigret.

'Mind you, I only mention it by way of a reminder. You are young and probably new in the job. You're lucky to have come across a friend of your chief's. I imagine you have good reason to enter this house as you have done. Louis told me about it. No doubt the individual he threw out is dangerous? Even so, young man, you could have waited until morning, don't you think? Do please sit down.'

He himself remained on his feet, pacing up and down and exhaling the smoke from his gold-tipped Egyptian cigarette.

'Now that I've taught you the little lesson you deserved, tell me what it is you wanted to know.'

'Whose is the bedroom upstairs?'

'I beg your pardon?'

'I'm sorry. I know you are under no obligation to reply, at least for the time being.'

'Obligation to . . .?' echoed Richard in utter amazement. And Maigret, his ears beetroot:

'A short while ago, a shot was fired in the bedroom.'

'What? . . . What . . . You are in your right mind, I hope? . . .'

'Even though it's been a night of street celebrations, I assume you haven't been drinking excessively?'

Footsteps could be heard on the stairs. The door had remained ajar, and Maigret glimpsed a new figure on the landing, a silhouette straight off the cover of *La Vie Parisienne*. The man was wearing a tailcoat, a cape and an opera hat. He was bony and elderly, and his thin moustache curling up at the ends was visibly dyed.

He hovered in the doorway, hesitant, surprised, perhaps afraid.

'Come in, father. Listen to this, it will make you laugh. Monsieur, here, is one of Le Bret's men . . .'

It was strange; Félicien Gendreau-Balthazar, the father, couldn't have been drunk, and yet there was something vague about him, something insubstantial, fluttery.

'Have you seen Louis?' his son continued.

'He's downstairs with someone.'

'Exactly. Earlier, a drunkard – unless he's a madman escaped from Villejuif – practically kicked the door down. Louis went down and had a terrible job keeping him out. And now, Monsieur—'

He paused with an inquiring look.

'Maigret.'

'Monsieur Maigret, who is the secretary to our friend Le Bret, is here to ask me . . . What was it exactly that you wanted to know?'

'Whose bedroom is above us, the one that has the second window on the left?'

He sensed that the father was worried, but it was a strange disquiet. For example, since his arrival the old man had been gazing at his son with a sort of fear, almost submissiveness. He didn't dare open his mouth. It was as if he were waiting for Richard's permission.

'It's my sister's,' Richard said at length. 'Now you know.'

'Is she in the house at the moment?'

And Maigret looked not at the son, but at the father. But once again, it was the son who replied.

'No. She is at Anseval.'

'I'm sorry?'

'Our chateau, the Château d'Anseval, near Pouilly-sur-Loire, in the Nièvre.'

'So the room is empty?'

'I have every reason to believe so.'

He added sarcastically:

'I imagine you would like to see for yourself. I'll show you up. Then tomorrow I shall be able to congratulate our friend Le Bret on the zeal of his subordinate. Please come this way.'

To Maigret's surprise, the father followed too, somewhat timorously.

'This is the room you mentioned. Fortunately it's not locked.'

He switched on the light. The furniture was of white lacquered wood, the walls covered in blue silk. A side door opened into a boudoir, and everything was in order, each object seemed to be in its rightful place.

'Carry out your search, I beg you. My sister will be delighted to know that the police have been poking their noses into her things.'

Unfazed, Maigret walked over to the window. The heavy silk curtains were of a darker blue than the walls. He opened them to find net curtains designed to soften daylight, and noticed that a corner of the netting was caught in the window.

'I don't suppose anyone has been in here this evening?' he asked.

'Unless one of the maids . . .'

'Are there several in the house?'

'Naturally!' sneered Richard. 'There are two, Germaine

and Marie. There's also Louis' wife, who is our cook, and there's even a laundress, but she's married and only comes in during the day.'

Félicien Gendreau, the father, kept glancing from one to the other.

'What is this about?' he asked eventually, after clearing his throat.

'I don't know exactly. Ask Monsieur Maigret.'

'Someone who was walking past the house just before one thirty heard this window opening. He looked up and saw a distraught woman who was shouting for help.'

Maigret noticed the father clench the gilt knob of his cane.

'And then what?' asked Richard.

'The woman was pulled backwards, and a gunshot rang out.'

'Really?'

The younger Gendreau looked about him with an expression of mock concern, pretending to try to find traces of a bullet on the silk walls.

'What I find surprising, Monsieur Maigret − it is Maigret, isn't it? − is that, given the seriousness of the accusation, you didn't take the elementary precaution of informing your superiors. You rushed straight here rather rashly, it seems to me. Did you take the trouble to find out anything about this passer-by who has such a fertile imagination?'

'He's downstairs.'

'I'm happy to hear that he is under my roof. In short, not only did you come in here in the middle of the night, in defiance of the law protecting civil liberties, but you have brought with you an individual whom I consider somewhat dubious, to say the least. But now you are here, please proceed with your routine search so that you can make a full report to our friend Le Bret tomorrow. I presume you want to ascertain that the bed hasn't been slept in tonight?'

He pulled back the satin bedspread to reveal sheets without a single crease, a pristine pillow.

'Take your time, please. Search every nook and cranny. I presume you have a magnifying glass?'

'I don't need one.'

'I'm sorry. Apart from Le Bret, my only acquaintance with the police is through novels. A shot was fired, you say? Maybe there's a body somewhere? Follow me. Let's hunt for it together! In this wardrobe perhaps? Who knows?'

He flung open the doors, but it contained nothing but dresses on hangers.

'In here? These are Lise's shoes. She's crazy about shoes, as you can see. Let's go into her boudoir . . .'

He was tense, becoming more and more sarcastic.

'This door? It has been boarded up since Mother's death. But we can enter the apartment from the corridor. Come. Oh yes, I insist . . .'

Maigret spent a nightmare half-hour. He had no option but to obey. For Richard was literally ordering him about. There was something spooky about the whole scene as they combed through the house followed closely by old Gendreau-Balthazar, who still had his opera hat on his head, his cape around his shoulders and his cane with its gilt knob in his hand.

'Oh no! We're not going downstairs yet. You're forgetting that there's a floor above us, an attic floor, where the servants sleep.'

The lightbulbs in the corridor were bare and the ceiling was slanted. Richard knocked on each door.

'Open the door, Germaine. Yes please! It doesn't matter if you're in your nightdress. It's the police.'

A plumpish girl who was half-asleep and gave off a musty smell, a damp bed, a comb clotted with hair on a dressing table.

'Did you hear a gunshot?'

'A what?'

'What time did you go to bed?'

'I came upstairs at ten o'clock.'

'And you didn't hear anything?'

Richard was asking all the questions.

'Next! . . . Open up, Marie . . . No, no, dear, it's not important . . .'

A girl of sixteen who had slipped a coat over her nightdress and was trembling from head to toe.

'Did you hear a gunshot?'

She stared at Richard and Maigret with a sort of terror.

'Have you been asleep long?'

'I don't know.'

'Did you hear anything?'

'No. Why? What's going on?'

'Any questions, Monsieur Maigret?'

'I'd like to ask her where she comes from.'

'Where do you come from, Marie?'

'From Anseval.'

'What about Germaine?'

'Also from Anseval.'

'And Louis?'

'From Anseval, Monsieur Maigret,' replied Richard with disdain. 'You are clearly unaware of the fact that people who own a chateau tend to hire their servants from the village.'

'The next door?'

'Madame Louis' room.'

'Does her husband sleep there too?'

'He sleeps downstairs, in the lodge.'

It took Madame Louis longer to open the door. She was short, swarthy and very fat, and had wary eyes.

'Have you finished making a racket? Where's Louis?'

'Downstairs. Tell me, did you hear a gunshot?'

She almost threw them out, muttering furiously. And Richard carried on opening more doors, into empty rooms, junk closets, garret rooms. Maigret wasn't spared the attic, and then he had to go down to the first floor and visit the apartments of the father and the son.

'There are still the drawing rooms. Oh yes, I absolutely insist.'

Richard switched on the great chandelier with tinkling crystal droplets.

'No dead body? No one wounded? Have you seen the whole house? Don't you want to go down into the cellar? You'll note that it is now a quarter past three.'

He opened the pantry door and they saw Justin Minard

sitting on a chair, with Louis standing in a corner guarding him as if he were a prisoner.

'Is this the young man who heard the shot? Delighted to have seen his interesting face. I presume, now, Monsieur Maigret, that I am entitled to file a complaint for slander and attempted forced entry.'

'You are indeed within your rights to do so.'

'I wish you good night. Louis, show these gentlemen out.'

Old Gendreau opened his mouth but said nothing. As for Maigret, he managed to say:

'Thank you very much.'

Louis walked close behind and shut the heavy door after them.

Disconcerted and slightly anxious, they were all alone on the left-hand pavement of Rue Chaptal. Maigret turned round automatically towards the patch of oil on the wooden paving, as if to grasp at something tangible in spite of everything.

'I swear I hadn't been drinking.'

'I believe you.'

'And I'm not mad.'

'Most certainly not.'

'Do you think this is going to get you into trouble? I vaguely heard . . .'

That night, Maigret's brand-new tailcoat was a little tight under the arms.

## 2. Richard's Lie

At 9.50 a smiling Madame Maigret smelling fragrant and fresh drew back the bedroom curtains to let in the bright sunlight. Newly married, she was not yet used to seeing a man asleep, with the tips of his reddish moustache quivering, his forehead creasing when a fly landed on it and his thick hair tousled. She laughed. She always laughed when she brought him a cup of coffee in the morning and he looked at her with hazy, slightly childlike eyes.

She was a plump, cheerful young woman, bursting with energy — the kind you see in bakeries or behind the marble counter of a dairy. He could leave her alone for days on end in their little apartment on Boulevard Richard-Lenoir and she wouldn't be bored for a second.

'What are you thinking about, Jules?'

In those days, she didn't call him Maigret, but she already had for him the sort of respect that he automatically inspired, the same respect she must have had for her father, the same she would have for her son, were she to have one.

'I'm thinking . . .'

And he recited the words that had come into his head on opening his eyes, after only two hours' sleep. They were extracts from the police manual:

*It is a hard-and-fast rule that agents of the Sûreté must devote*
*all their time to their duties.*

*Any investigation or surveillance operation undertaken*
*must, in principle, be conducted continually; leave cannot be*
*guaranteed at fixed hours or even on fixed days.*

He had left the police station at six in the morning, when
the deputy secretary, Albert Luce, had come on duty. The
air outside was chilly and the streets of Paris so filled with
aromas that he had walked home and had been tempted
to make a detour via Les Halles to relish the smell of spring
vegetables and fruits.

At present, there were hundreds, thousands of people in
Paris who had not had much more sleep than him. Although
the foreign sovereign's visit was to last only three days, the
police were under a lot of pressure, and some squads, like
those in charge of security, the railway stations, aliens and
traffic duty had been on high alert for weeks.

Men were seconded from various departments and
from local police stations. The king's strictly scheduled
comings and goings did not affect the Saint-Georges
district, so all available men had been sent to the Opéra
police station.

It wasn't just the anarchists who were giving the police
a headache. There were the madmen who invariably went
berserk during this sort of grand occasion; there were the
pickpockets and swindlers who were having a field day
with the provincials flocking to the capital to watch the
parades.

'Is it Balthazar coffee?' he asked.

'Why do you ask? Don't you like it?'

'I wanted to know what made you buy this coffee rather than another one. Is it because it's better?'

'It's not bad at any rate, and there are the picture cards.'

He had forgotten about the albums into which she carefully pasted the pictures of all the different species of flowers that came inside the packets of coffee.

'When you have three complete sets, you win a walnut bedroom suite.'

Since they didn't have a bathroom in the apartment yet, Maigret had a sponge bath, then he ate some soup for breakfast, as he had always done at home in the country.

'I don't suppose you know what time you'll be back?'

And he repeated, smiling:

'. . . *leave cannot be guaranteed at fixed hours or even on fixed days.*'

She knew it by heart. She already had her hat on. She liked walking with him to his office, as if taking a child to school, but she didn't go all the way as he would have been embarrassed to run into a colleague.

On the dot of ten, the chief inspector's gig drew up in Rue de La-Rochefoucauld, the horse pawing at the ground as the coachman took over the reins from his master. Maxime Le Bret was probably the only police inspector in Paris to have his own carriage and live in the Plaine-Monceau neighbourhood, in one of the new apartment buildings on Boulevard de Courcelles.

By the time he arrived in style at the police station, he had already dropped into the Hoche club for a bout of fencing, a swim in the pool and a relaxing massage.

Maigret's report was on his desk, and Maigret thought about it with a gnawing anxiety. This was his first important report and he had painstakingly worked on it until dawn, trying not to leave out any of the hypotheses still fresh in his mind.

The flautist, Justin Minard, had walked back from Rue Chaptal to the police station with him. They paused outside the door.

'Are you married?' asked Maigret.

'Yes.'

'Don't you think your wife will be worried?'

'It doesn't matter.'

And Justin had come in. Maigret had taken his statement, which the musician had signed. He still wouldn't leave.

'Don't you think your wife will make a scene?'

And again Minard said softly:

'It doesn't matter.'

Why was Maigret remembering this now? He had almost had to show him the door at daybreak. And again the flautist had asked, with a mixture of shyness and assurance:

'May I come and see you?'

He had filed a complaint against the man named Louis. He had insisted. All the paperwork was in order on the chief inspector's desk, on top of less important daily reports.

Maigret never saw Maxime Le Bret come in because he went down the corridor straight into his office, but he could hear him, and this time his heart skipped a beat.

On the bench sat the usual motley assortment of regular

customers, mainly sad souls and poor bedraggled wretches. He called out their names one by one, provided them with certificates of residence or of hardship, made a note of items that had been lost or found, and sent the vagrants and hawkers who had been picked up on the streets down to the lock-up.

Just below the black-rimmed clock there was an electric bell, and, when that bell rang . . .

He had calculated that it would take Le Bret about twelve minutes to read his report and Minard's statement. Twenty minutes went by and Le Bret still hadn't called him in, but a soft click told him that his boss was making a telephone call.

There was a baize door between Le Bret's office and the main office. A murmur from the other side was faintly audible.

Was Le Bret already speaking to Richard Gendreau, who so frequently invited him to dine at his house?

No bell, but the door opened.

'Maigret!'

A good sign or a bad sign?

'Come in, my boy.'

The chief inspector paced up and down the room, smoking a cigarette before sitting down at his desk. Eventually, he placed his hand on the file and appeared to be casting around for the right words.

'I've read that thing of yours,' he sighed.

'Yes, sir.'

'You did what you believed was right. Your report is very clear, very detailed.'

'Thank you, sir.'

'It even mentions me.'

He raised a hand to silence Maigret, who had opened his mouth to speak.

'I am not criticizing you at all. On the contrary.'

'I did my best to transcribe faithfully everything that was said.'

'In short, you were able to look around the entire house at your leisure.'

'They showed me every room.'

'You were able to ascertain that there was nothing untoward.'

'In the bedroom mentioned by Justin Minard, the net curtain was caught in the window as if it had been closed hastily.'

'That can happen at any time, can't it? Nothing proves that the curtain hadn't been like that for several days.'

'The father, Monsieur Félicien Gendreau-Balthazar, seemed very perturbed by my presence in the house.'

'You wrote *frightened*.'

'That was the feeling I had.'

'I know Gendreau personally. I meet him several times a week at my club.'

'I know, sir.'

The chief inspector was a handsome man with a patrician manner. He was to be found at all the society gatherings, having married a wealthy Parisian heiress. That was probably why, despite his lifestyle, he insisted on having a regular job. His eyelids had fine creases and there were deep crow's feet around his eyes. He had probably had no more sleep than Maigret the previous night, or any other night.

'Call Besson in, would you.'

Besson was an inspector, the only one who had remained at the station during the royal visit.

'I have a little job for you, Besson, my man.'

He copied out the name and address of Justin Minard, the flautist, on to a loose sheet of paper.

'I want you to make some discreet inquiries about this gentleman. The sooner the better.'

Besson looked at the address, was pleased to see that it was in Paris and promised:

'Right away, sir.'

And, when Le Bret was alone again with Maigret, he smiled very faintly and said:

'Right. I think that's all there is to be done for the time being.'

Sitting at his black desk, Maigret spent the most furious hours of his life examining grubby documents, listening to concierges' complaints and street hawkers' excuses.

He thought of various extreme options, such as handing in his notice immediately.

So according to the chief inspector, all that needed to be done was to make inquiries about the flautist! Why not arrest him and give him a going over?

Maigret could also have telephoned the big chief, Xavier Guichard, or gone to see him, since he knew the head of the Sûreté personally. The latter had often spent his holidays near their home in the Allier, and he had once been a friend of his father's.

He hadn't exactly taken Maigret under his wing, but he kept an avuncular eye on him from a distance, or rather from on high, and it was probably thanks to him that over the past four years Maigret had constantly been transferred between departments so that he could become acquainted with all the workings of the police within a short space of time.

'Minard isn't mad. He wasn't drunk. He saw a window open. He heard a shot. And I saw those patches of oil on the road for myself.'

That's what he would say, outraged. He would insist . . .

That gave him an idea and he left the room, going down three steps into the duty office where uniformed officers were playing cards.

'Tell me, sergeant, have all the men who were on duty last night already made their reports?'

'Not all.'

'Would you ask them something? I'd like to know whether any of them noticed a De Dion-Bouton in the neighbourhood between midnight and two in the morning. The driver was wearing a grey goatskin jacket and huge goggles. I don't know if there were any passengers.'

Too bad for the chief inspector! *Any investigation or surveillance undertaken . . .*

He knew his theory. Ordinarily, this would be his case, Balthazar or no Balthazar.

At around midday he began to feel sleepy, but it wasn't his turn to go for lunch yet. His eyelids were pricking. He caught himself repeating the same question twice while interrogating his customers.

Besson came back, the smell of absinthe clinging to his moustache, and that made Maigret hanker for the coolness of a café or the subdued light of a terrace on the boulevards.

'Is the chief still here?'

He had left, and Besson sat down to write his report.

'Poor fellow!' he sighed.

'Who?'

'The musician.'

And Besson, who exuded health with his soft, glowing skin, went on:

'To start with, he's consumptive, which is no fun. They've been trying to send him to the mountains for two years, but he won't hear of it.'

Horses clattered across Place Saint-Georges. That morning there had been a military parade at Les Invalides and the troops from the various barracks were on their way back to their quarters. The city was still in ferment, with flags, uniforms, music and parades, dignitaries in colourful outfits hastening to the Élysée where there was a big state banquet.

'They live in a two-room apartment overlooking the courtyard, on the fifth floor with no lift.'

'Did you go up?'

'I talked to the coal merchant who lives in the building, then to the concierge, who's from my part of the world. Every month she gets complaints from the residents, because he plays the flute all day long with the windows

29

wide open. The concierge is fond of him. So is the coal merchant, even though Minard owes him for two or three months' worth of coal. As for his missus—'

'Did you see her?'

'She walked past when I was in the concierge's lodge. A big brunette on the heavy side with flashing eyes. A sort of Carmen. Always in her dressing gown and slippers, hanging around in the local shops. She has her cards read. She yells at him. The concierge claims she even beats him. Poor fellow!'

Besson laboriously penned a few lines – writing reports wasn't his strong point.

'I took the Métro and I went to see Minard's boss at the Brasserie Clichy. Nothing to report. He doesn't drink. He always arrives five minutes early. He's nice to everybody and the girl on the till adores him.'

'Where was he this morning?'

'I don't know. Not at home. The concierge would have told me if he had been.'

Maigret left the office to go and eat two hard-boiled eggs and drink a beer in a little café on Place Saint-Georges. When he came back, he found a note from the sergeant on his desk.

*Officer Jullian noticed the presence of a De Dion-Bouton motorcar at 1.30 a.m. It was parked in Rue Mansart, outside number 28. The only occupant was the driver who matches the description given. The vehicle remained in Rue Mansart for approximately ten minutes and drove off in the direction of Rue Blanche.*

The bell under the clock rang, and Maigret leaped up to open the baize door. Le Bret was already back, and Maigret could see the pages of his report spread over the desk, with annotations in red pencil.

'Come in, dear boy. Have a seat.'

This was a rare favour, as the chief inspector usually left his men standing.

'I imagine you have spent all morning cursing me?'

He too was in a tailcoat, but his came from the best tailor on Place Vendôme and his waistcoats were always in the softest colours.

'I've re-read your report thoroughly. A very good report, by the way, as I think I already told you. I also had a conversation with Besson about your friend the flautist.'

Maigret felt emboldened.

'Have the Gendreau-Balthazars telephoned you?'

'They have indeed, but not to complain, if that's what you think. Richard Gendreau was perfectly amicable. Actually, he was rather amused by you and your zeal! No doubt you were expecting recriminations from him? It was quite the opposite. I don't suppose you'll be surprised that he considers you to be young and impetuous. That is precisely why he took a perverse pleasure in opening every door of his house to you.'

Maigret was frowning, and his boss watched him with a slight smile, the blasé smile that was the hallmark of the 'fast set', as they were called.

'Now tell me, my boy, if you were in my shoes, what would you have done this morning?'

And, since Maigret said nothing, he went on:

'Apply for a search warrant? First of all, on what grounds? Has a complaint been filed? Not against the Gendreaus, in any case. Has a crime been committed? None. Has anyone been injured, is there a body? Not as far as we know. And you visited the house last night and went over it with a fine-tooth comb, you saw everyone who lives there, some of them in their night clothes.

'Don't get me wrong. I am perfectly aware of what must have been going through your mind all day. I am a friend of the Gendreaus. I am a regular guest at their home. I belong to the same social circle as they do. Admit that you've been cursing me.'

'There is Minard's statement and complaint.'

'The flautist. I'm coming to him. At around one thirty this morning, he tried to force his way into a private residence claiming that he had heard a woman cry for help.'

'He saw—'

'Don't forget that he is the only person to have seen anything, that no neighbours were disturbed. Put yourself in the place of the butler who was woken up by someone trying to kick the door down.'

'Excuse me! The butler, Louis, was fully dressed, tie and all, at one thirty this morning even though at the hour Minard rang the bell the house was in total darkness.'

'Be that as it may. Note that it's your flautist again who stated that the butler was fully dressed. But is that a crime? Minard was thrown out fairly violently. But what would you do if a dubious individual were to burst in on you in the middle of the night claiming that you were murdering your wife?'

He proffered a gold cigarette case and Maigret had to remind him for the umpteenth time that he didn't smoke cigarettes. It was a mannerism of Le Bret's, a gesture of aristocratic condescension.

'Let us look at the matter from a strictly administrative point of view. You have written a report, which must go through the usual channels, i.e. it will be passed on to the commissioner, who will decide whether to pass it on to the prosecutor. The flautist's complaint against the butler will also be processed in the usual way.'

Maigret glared at him steadily and once again considered handing in his notice. He guessed what was coming next.

'The Gendreau-Balthazars are one of the most prominent Paris families. If the slightest indiscretion were committed, every sordid blackmailing scandal sheet would jump at the opportunity.'

Maigret snapped:

'I understand.'

'And you hate me, isn't that so? You think I'm protecting these people because they're powerful or because they're my friends.'

Maigret made to gather the papers on the desk and tear them up as was expected of him. Then he would go back to the main office and write his letter of resignation, in a handwriting that was as firm as possible.

'Now, young Maigret, I have some news for you.'

It was odd, Le Bret's mocking tone had become affectionate.

'This morning, while I was reading your report, and

then again while I was talking to you, something was niggling me. Like a vague memory. I don't know if you ever experience that. The harder you try to pin it down, the hazier it becomes. But I knew it was important, that it could even shed an entirely new light on things. And then I finally put my finger on it, just before going to lunch. Contrary to my usual habit, I ate lunch at home because we had guests. As I looked at my wife, I found one of the links. The thing that had been niggling me all morning was something she had said, but what? Suddenly, in the middle of lunch, it came back to me. Yesterday, before leaving Boulevard de Courcelles, I asked, as I often do: "What are you doing this afternoon?" and my wife replied: "I'm going to have tea in Faubourg Saint-Honoré with Lise and Bernadette." Bernadette is the Countess d'Estirau. And Lise is Lise Gendreau-Balthazar.'

He stopped and looked at Maigret, a twinkle in his eyes.

'There, my boy. All I needed to do was check whether Lise Gendreau really did have tea with my wife at five o'clock in the Pihan tearooms. She did, my wife confirmed. At no point did she say she was going to Anseval. When I got back to the office, I re-read your report carefully.'

Maigret's face lit up and he had already opened his mouth to speak.

'Just a moment! Not so fast. Last night, you found this same Lise Gendreau's bedroom empty. Her brother told you she had gone to the Nièvre.'

'So—'

'That proves nothing. Richard Gendreau wasn't speaking

under oath. You had no search warrant, no grounds for questioning him.'

'But now—'

'None now, either. That is why I'm advising you . . .'

Maigret was at a loss to understand. His heart sank, and he wasn't sure what to do or say. He was hot. He felt humiliated by being treated like a child.

'Have you already made your holiday plans?'

He nearly gave a rude reply.

'I know that public servants are in the habit of arranging their days off and annual leave well in advance. However, you may take your holiday as of today if you wish. I think that will even ease my conscience. Especially if you were not intending to leave Paris. A police officer on leave is no longer a police officer, and there are steps he can permit himself to take that it would be difficult to sanction officially.'

Hope again. But Maigret was still afraid. He was expecting another volte-face.

'Of course I hope I won't receive any complaints about you. Should you have something to tell me, or should you need any information, you can call me at home, Boulevard de Courcelles. You'll find my number in the telephone directory.'

Maigret opened his mouth once again, this time to say thank you, but the chief inspector, who was gently shooing him towards the door, suddenly recalled a minor detail, and added:

'Actually, six or seven years ago, Félicien Gendreau – the

father – appointed a board of trustees, as if he were some hare-brained young man. And it's Richard who, since his mother's death, has effectively been in control of the family's affairs. Is your wife well? Is she becoming accustomed to living in Paris and her new apartment?'

A dry handshake and Maigret found himself on the other side of the baize door. Still dazed, he was making his way mechanically over to his black desk when his gaze fell on one of the figures sitting on the bench on the other side of what they called the counter.

It was Justin Minard the flautist, all in black though not evening dress this time, and minus his beige overcoat. He was sitting quietly, sandwiched between a tramp and a fat woman with a green shawl who was breastfeeding her baby.

The musician winked at him, as if to ask if he could come up to the barrier. Maigret gave him a little nod of recognition, tidied away his papers, and briefed one of his colleagues on various cases in hand.

'I'm on leave!' he announced.

'Leave, in April, with a visiting monarch to deal with?'

'Leave.'

And the colleague, who knew that Maigret had recently married:

'Baby?'

'No baby.'

'Ill?'

'Not ill.'

That was more than worrying, and the colleague shook his head.

'Well, it's none of my business! Have a good holiday anyway. Some people have all the luck.'

Maigret picked up his hat, put on his cuffs – which he had removed on arriving at the office – and went through the gate that separated the police officers from the public. Justin Minard rose quite naturally and, just as naturally, he followed Maigret outside without saying a word.

Had he received a thrashing from his wife, as Besson had suggested? He stood there, fair-haired and frail, with rosy cheeks and blue eyes, keeping close to Maigret like a stray dog who latches on to a passer-by.

The sun was streaming down and there were flags in every window. The air seemed to reverberate with the sound of drums and bugles. The crowds were exuberant and most of the men held themselves upright like soldiers, inspired by the military parades.

When at last Minard drew level with Maigret and walked alongside him, he asked him nervously:

'Have you been fired?'

He thought, of course, that a public servant could be fired as easily as a flautist and he was distressed to think that he was the cause.

'I haven't been fired. I'm on leave.'

'Oh!'

His 'Oh!' was uneasy. It contained an anxiety, already almost a reproach.

'They'd rather you weren't there for the time being, is that it? I assume they're going to drop the case, and my complaint?'

His tone hardened.

'They're not going to ignore my complaint, I hope? I'm telling you now that I won't let them walk all over me.'

'The complaint will go through the usual channels.'

'Good! Especially since I've got some news for you. Well, one piece of news . . .'

They had reached Place Saint-Georges, a quiet, provincial little square with a café that smelled of white wine. Maigret, unable to resist, pushed open the door. There was a festive atmosphere that afternoon. The pewter counter had been freshly polished and the Vouvray shimmered pale green in the glasses, making Maigret feel thirsty.

'You saw two maids in the house, didn't you? That's what you told me, right?'

'Germaine and Marie,' Maigret reeled off. 'As well as Madame Louis, the cook.'

'Well, in fact there was only one!'

The musician's eyes lit up with childlike glee, making him look even more like an affectionate dog who had retrieved a stick for its master.

'I had a chat with the woman at the dairy where the Gendreaus buy their milk, just next to the tobacconist's on the corner of Rue Fontaine.'

Maigret stared at him in amazement, slightly embarrassed, and he couldn't help thinking of him being thrashed by that Carmen creature.

'Since Saturday, Germaine, the eldest maid, has been in the Oise, where her sister is about to give birth. I'm completely free during the day, you see?'

'What about your wife?'

'It doesn't matter,' he repeated in a slightly distant voice. 'I said to myself that if you're carrying on with the investigation, I could perhaps help you out a little. People are generally nice to me. I don't know why.'

And Maigret thought: 'Except for Carmen!'

'Now it's my round. Yes, I insist. Just because I drink strawberry cordial, it doesn't mean I can't buy a round. You're not really on leave, are you? That was a joke, wasn't it?'

Was it breaking professional secrecy to wink?

'I'd have been disappointed if you'd said you were. I don't know those people. I have nothing against them personally. But the fact is that Louis is a thug and they lied.'

A little girl in red was selling mimosa freshly arrived from Nice, and Maigret bought a bunch for his wife, who only knew the Riviera from a colour picture postcard of the Baie des Anges.

'Just tell me what I have to do. And please, don't be afraid that I'll bring you trouble! I'm used to shutting up and keeping quiet!'

His eyes were beseeching. He would have liked to buy Maigret another Vouvray to convince him, but he didn't dare.

'Those houses always conceal dark secrets, only there are some who are in the know. The servants usually talk too much, and the tradesmen are a mine of information.'

Without thinking, unaware that in a way he was sealing his partnership with the flautist, Maigret muttered:

'Mademoiselle Gendreau is not at Anseval, as her brother claimed.'

'So where is she?'

'Since Germaine was away, it was probably Lise Gendreau that I saw in the maid's room, in her nightdress.'

That made Maigret uneasy. He had spent his childhood in the shadow of a chateau where his father had been the estate manager. As a result, he had acquired a respect for people in high places, the rich. And strangest of all was that the flautist shared his embarrassment. He said nothing for a good while but sat staring at his strawberry cordial.

'Do you think so?' he asked at length, troubled.

'In any case, there was a woman in a nightdress in the maid's room. A plump girl with a stale smell.'

And that also troubled him, as if young ladies from good families whose names are plastered all over the corridors of the Métro in capital letters weren't capable of smelling stale like farm girls.

The two men sitting in front of their drinks, the scent of mimosa mingling with that of white wine and strawberries, the sun on the backs of their necks, were both lost in a vague dream, and Maigret started when his companion's voice brought him back down to earth. Justin Minard was saying, his voice completely guileless:

'Now what do we do?'

# 3. A Few Rounds with Old Paumelle

*Police officers are advised to own a black dress suit, a dinner jacket and a morning coat, without which it is not possible to gain admission to some society gatherings.*

This was one of the instructions that were as fresh in his memory as the catechism is in the mind of a boy making his first communion. But the recommendations were rather over-optimistic. Or otherwise the word 'some' needed further qualification.

He had tried on his dress suit the previous evening with the idea of gaining entry to the circles frequented by the Gendreaus, the Hoche club, for example, or the Haussmann, but one little comment from his wife had been enough to bring him back down to earth.

'You're so handsome, Jules!' she had exclaimed as he inspected his reflection in the wardrobe mirror.

She would never have taken the liberty of laughing at him. She was certainly speaking in earnest. All the same there was something indefinable in her tone, in her smile, that warned him not to try to pass himself off as a young clubman.

Resting their elbows on the window ledge, they could hear the sounds of a torchlight retreat coming from Place de la Bastille. As the coolness of the night enveloped them, Maigret was finding it hard to remain positive.

'You see, if I crack this case, it's almost a guaranteed passport to Quai des Orfèvres. Once I'm there . . .'

What more could he want? To be part of the Sûreté, perhaps the famous murder squad, dubbed the chief's squad!

But to get there he had to bring this case to a successful conclusion – in other words, without drawing attention to himself – and uncover the darkest secrets of a wealthy household in Rue Chaptal.

He spent a restless night and, on waking at six o'clock in the morning, he was once again presented with an ironic reminder of his police manual.

*A cap, a scarf and a worn jacket prove to be a very effective disguise.*

This time, as he inspected his reflection in the mirror, Madame Maigret hadn't laughed but said affectionately:

'Next month you really must buy yourself a suit.'

She was tactfully trying to say that his tatty old jacket was hardly more tired than his so-called 'best' suit. In other words, he had no need for a disguise.

So he ended up putting on his collar and tie as well as his bowler hat.

The weather was still magnificent, as if in honour of the visiting sovereign, who would be driven to Versailles later that day. Nearly two hundred thousand Parisians were already on their way to the royal town, whose parks by evening would be strewn with greasy wrappers and empty bottles.

Meanwhile, Justin Minard would be taking the train to Conflans where he planned to track down the famous Germaine, the Gendreaus' maid.

'If I can just find her,' he had said with his disarming gentleness, 'I'm sure she'll tell me everything she knows. I have no idea why, but people always seem to want to tell me their life story.'

It was seven o'clock when Maigret took possession, as it were, of Rue Chaptal, and he was glad he hadn't worn a cap and scarf, since the first person he met was an officer from his station who greeted him by name.

There are bustling streets full of shops and cafés where it is easy to blend in, but Rue Chaptal is not one of them. Short and wide, it has no shops and very few people use it.

All the curtains of the Gendreau-Balthazar mansion were tightly drawn, as in most of the other houses in the street. Maigret loitered on one corner and then another, feeling rather conspicuous. When a maid came out of one of the buildings to go and fetch the milk from the dairy in Rue Fontaine, next to the tobacconist's, he had the impression that she was looking at him with suspicion and that she hastened her step.

It was the worst time of day. Despite the sunshine, there was still a nip in the air, and he had not worn his overcoat, as it would be hot later. The pavements were absolutely empty. The tobacconist's on the corner didn't open until 7.30, when Maigret went in and drank a foul cup of coffee that made his stomach heave.

Another maid with her milk-can, then another. They looked as if they had just got out of bed and hadn't washed yet. Then shutters opened here and there, and women with their hair in curling papers gazed out into the street, invariably eyeing him with suspicion. But there was no movement at the Gendreaus'; it wasn't until 8.30 that a chauffeur in a very tight-fitting black uniform arrived from Rue Notre-Dame-de-Lorette and rang the bell.

Luckily the Vieux Calvados on the corner of Rue Henner, almost opposite the Gendreaus', had just opened. It was the only place in the street that offered Maigret a refuge. He stepped inside in the nick of time.

Louis, wearing a striped waistcoat, opened the door then exchanged a few words with the driver. The door stayed open, as it would do all day. Beyond the porch, Maigret glimpsed a sun-drenched courtyard, some foliage, a garage, and the sound of hooves suggested that there were also stables.

'Are you wanting to eat?'

A very fat man with a very ruddy face and beady little eyes was calmly eyeing Maigret, who jumped.

'What say you to a few slices of *andouille* with a bowl of cider? It's the best way to start the day.'

And that was how Maigret's day began, one that was typical of many that he would experience during his career but which, at this early stage, felt like a dream.

The place itself was rather extraordinary. In this street of private mansions and expensive apartment buildings, the Vieux Calvados looked like a country inn that had been forgotten when Paris had spread. The building was low and narrow with a little step down into a rather dark, very cool room with a dull pewter counter. The bottles looked as if they had been standing there for ever.

There was a special smell too. It came perhaps from the open trap door in the floor that led down to the cellar.

A sort of acidic cloud wafted up from below – cider mingled with calvados, old barrels and must – while cooking aromas came from the kitchen. At the back of the room, a spiral staircase led up to the mezzanine, and the whole effect was that of a stage set. The owner, stubby-legged, very broad, with an obstinate forehead and a glint in his eyes, paced up and down like an actor.

Did Maigret have any alternative but to accept what was put in front of him? He had never drunk cider at breakfast. This was his first experience and, contrary to his expectations, he felt a warm glow in his chest.

'I'm waiting for someone,' he ventured by way of an explanation.

'It's no business of mine!'

But the shrug of his massive shoulders said: 'I don't believe you!'

There was a cynical glint in his eyes, so cynical that after a while Maigret began to feel uncomfortable.

The owner ate too, at the bar, thick slices of *andouille* and after a quarter of an hour he had drained the jug of cider drawn from the barrel in the cellar.

Over the road at the Gendreaus', Maigret caught an occasional glimpse of the chauffeur in the courtyard. He had removed his jacket and was busy hosing down a car of which only the front wheels were visible. But it wasn't a De Dion-Bouton. It was a black limousine with huge copper headlamps.

There were still few passers-by in the street – a handful of workers heading towards the Métro, maids or house-wives hurrying to the shops in Rue Fontaine.

Nobody came into the Vieux Calvados, where an enormous woman appeared on the spiral staircase, her feet coming into view first, encased in red slippers. Without saying a word, she went into the kitchen.

*Officers on a surveillance operation are no longer their own masters: their actions are determined by the behaviour of the individual under surveillance.*

Curtains opened on the first floor, those of Richard Gendreau's bedroom. It was nine o'clock. The owner of the Vieux Calvados pottered about, a cloth in his hand, and seemed deliberately to be avoiding making conversation.

'It looks as if my friend's been delayed,' said Maigret, anxious to keep up appearances.

The Vieux Calvados wasn't a bar but a restaurant with a regular clientele. The red gingham tablecloths matched the curtains. Cooking aromas were already drifting through the doorway at the back and potatoes could be heard plopping into a bucket one at a time as they were peeled.

Why did the owner and his wife not speak to one another? Since the woman had come downstairs, the two of them – or rather the three of them – seemed to be acting out a strange pantomime.

The owner carried on wiping his bottles and glasses and polishing the pewter counter. He lingered for a moment in front of a row of earthenware jugs and eventually chose one. Then he promptly filled two glasses, jerked his head in the direction of the wall clock, next to a promotional calendar, and said simply:

'Time for a drink.'

His beady eyes on Maigret to see how he would react to the calvados, he clicked his tongue and picked up his cloth, which he looped through his braces when he wasn't using it.

At 9.30, the chauffeur over the road put on his jacket and the engine could be heard spluttering into action. The car pulled up beneath the porch, and a few minutes later Richard Gendreau, in a grey suit with a carnation in his buttonhole, clambered in.

Was the restaurant owner simply a mischievous fool? Or, on the contrary, had he already guessed everything? He glanced at the car as it drove past, then at Maigret, and then gave a gentle sigh and went back to work.

A quarter of an hour later, he resumed his place behind the bar, selected another jug, filled two little glasses without saying a word and nudged one towards his customer.

It was only later that Maigret gathered that this was a ritual, a kind of foible. Every half-hour, there was a little glass of calvados, which explained the man's blotchy complexion and rheumy eyes.

'Thank you, but . . .'

Too bad! It was impossible to say no. There was such authority in the insistent gaze fixed on him that he preferred to knock back the drink. He was beginning to feel tipsy.

At ten o'clock, he asked:

'Do you have a telephone?'

'Upstairs, opposite the WC.'

Maigret went up the spiral staircase into a little low-ceilinged room where there were only four tables with gingham cloths. The windows began at floor level.

Balthazar Coffee . . . Avenue de l'Opéra . . . Warehouses . . . Quai de Valmy . . . Head Office . . . Rue Auber . . .

He called head office.

'May I speak to Monsieur Richard Gendreau?'

'Who's calling?'

'Tell him that it's Louis.'

Almost immediately he recognized Gendreau's voice on the other end.

'Hello! Louis?'

He sounded anxious. Maigret hung up. Through the window he could see the butler in his striped waistcoat stationed on the pavement, where he was calmly smoking a cigarette. He didn't stay there for long. He must have heard the telephone ring.

Alarmed, his boss was calling him.

Good! So Richard Gendreau was at his office, where he probably spent the greater part of his time. Louis did not come back outside, but the main door stayed open.

A very young face appeared at a second-floor window where the curtains had just been drawn back. It was Marie, the little maid with a pointed nose, a neck like a plucked bird's and dishevelled hair beneath a pretty lace cap. She was wearing a soubrette's black dress and white apron.

He was afraid of staying upstairs too long and arousing the owner's suspicions. He came down just in time for the third calvados, which the owner poured with the same authority as before. As he gave him the glass, he pushed towards him a saucer on which there were slices of *andouille*, stating:

'I'm from Pontfarcy!'

He pronounced the word with such solemnity that it must have contained some mysterious significance. Did that explain the *andouille*? Were people from Pontfarcy in the habit of knocking back a glass of calvados every half-hour? He added:

'Near Vire!'

'May I make another telephone call?'

It wasn't yet 10.30 and Maigret was already familiar with the place. He was beginning to feel at home, and his mood was even fairly cheerful. The floor-to-ceiling window was entertaining as it allowed passers-by in the street below to peer in and see the diners.

'Hello! Is that Monsieur Gendreau-Balthazar's residence?'

This time it was Louis' lugubrious voice that answered.

'May I speak to Mademoiselle Gendreau, please?'

'Mademoiselle is not at home. Who's calling?'

Maigret hung up, as he had done before, and went back downstairs where the owner, concentrating hard, was writing out the day's menu on a slate, thinking carefully about each word.

There were a lot of open windows now, with rugs being beaten above the empty street. An elderly lady in black, wearing a hat with a purple veil, was walking a little dog which stopped at every doorway to raise its hind leg, in vain.

'I'm beginning to wonder,' mumbled Maigret with a forced laugh, 'whether my friend has forgotten that we're meeting.'

Did the owner believe him? Had he guessed that Maigret was from the police?

At eleven o'clock, he watched a coachman hitch a bay horse to a brougham in the courtyard of the Gendreaus' residence. But this coachman had not come in through the carriage entrance. He was unlikely to have slept in the house, which suggested that there was another way out of the property.

At 11.15, Félicien Gendreau, the father, came down dressed in a morning coat, yellow gloves, beige hat, cane in hand, his moustache neatly waxed. The coachman helped him clamber into the carriage, which set off in the direction of Rue Blanche. The elderly gentleman was probably going for a ride in the Bois de Boulogne before having luncheon at his club.

*. . . Police officers are advised to own a black dress suit, a dinner jacket and a morning coat . . .*

And Maigret, looking at himself in the mirror, surrounded by bottles, had a wry smile. And yellow gloves too, I suppose? And a cane with a gold knob! And light-coloured spats and patent-leather shoes!

Just his luck, for his first investigation! He could have

been required to infiltrate any milieu – petty bourgeois, shopkeepers, ragmen, vagrants. Any of those would have been easy but not this private mansion, its carriage entrance more imposing than a church door with its marble peristyle, and even its courtyard where a driver was polishing a limousine for one of the masters before harnessing a pedigree horse for the other!

Calvados! He had no choice. He would hold out until the end and remain at his post in the Vieux Calvados for as long as was necessary.

He hadn't caught sight of Madame Louis. Maybe she didn't do her shopping every morning, she probably had provisions at home, and the gentlemen must be having luncheon out.

Justin Minard was lucky. He was in the country now, tracking down Germaine Babœuf – he'd found out her surname from the dairy woman – who was at her sister's, probably in a humble little shack with a garden and chickens.

'Don't you think your wife . . .'

'It doesn't matter.'

And Madame Maigret who had decided to give the apartment a thorough spring clean today!

'Do you think it's worth it?' he had asked her. 'We won't be staying here for long. We're bound to find a place in a nicer neighbourhood soon.'

He couldn't know that, thirty years later, they would still be living in the same home on Boulevard Richard-Lenoir, having acquired the next-door apartment too.

At half past eleven, some customers walked into the

Vieux Calvados at last, painters in white overalls who were clearly regulars, since one of them greeted the owner with a familiar:

'*Salut*, Paumelle!'

For them, this was an aperitif, which they drank as they stood reading the menu slate before going to sit at a window table.

By midday all the tables were full. Every so often, Madame Paumelle would emerge from her kitchen carrying plates while her husband served the drinks, going up and down the stairs from the cellar to the ground floor and from the ground floor to the mezzanine. Most of the customers were workers from the nearby building sites, but there were also two cabmen whose carriages stood outside the restaurant.

Maigret would have liked to telephone Monsieur Le Bret to ask his advice. He had eaten and drunk too much. He felt sluggish and, if he had been in the Oise in the flautist's shoes, he would probably have indulged in a little nap in a field, under a tree, with a newspaper spread over his face.

His self-confidence was beginning to dwindle, as was his faith in his profession which, at times, felt futile. Was it a manly job idling the day away in a café, watching a house where nothing was happening? The other people there all had a specific job. All over Paris, people were coming and going like ants, but at least they knew where they were going!

No one was forced, for example, to drink a glass of calvados every half-hour, with a man whose eyes were growing increasingly unfocused, his smile increasingly sinister.

Paumelle was laughing at him, he was certain of it. But what else could he do? Go and stand outside, in the bright sunlight, in full view of the many windows overlooking the street?

The thought brought back an unpleasant memory, a stupid episode barely two years earlier that had almost made him leave the police. He had been put on patrol, with specific responsibility for pickpockets in the Métro.

*A cap, a scarf and a worn jacket are . . .*

In those days, he believed in his job. Deep down, he still did. The incident had happened opposite La Samaritaine. He'd been coming up the stairs from the Métro. Just in front of him, a man in a bowler hat deftly sliced the strap of an elderly lady's reticule. Maigret leaped at him, grabbed the black velvet bag and tried to hold on to the man, who started yelling:

'Stop thief!'

And the crowd had set upon Maigret with fists flying, while the man in the bowler hat discreetly slipped away.

Now he was beginning to have doubts about his friend, Justin Minard. Maybe the second-floor window had been opened, but so what? Everybody was entitled to open their window in the middle of the night. There are people who sleepwalk, who start shouting . . .

The Vieux Calvados had emptied. The owner and his wife hadn't exchanged a single word all day. They each went about their jobs in silence, as in a perfectly choreographed ballet.

And then at last, at 2.20, something happened. A car came cruising leisurely down the street, and it was a grey De Dion-Bouton. The man at the wheel was wearing a grey goatskin jacket and goggles.

The car did not stop in front of the Gendreau residence, but drove slowly past, and Maigret could see that there were no passengers. He rushed over to the window and managed to make a note of the registration number: *B780*.

He couldn't possibly run after the car, which turned into Rue Fontaine. He stood there, his heart racing, and less than five minutes later, the same car cruised past again.

When he returned to the bar, Paumelle stared fixedly at him, giving no indication of what he was thinking. He merely filled two glasses and pushed one towards his customer.

The car did not reappear. It was the hour when the Opéra's nymph-like corps de ballet was performing in the gardens of Versailles, all those gentlemen in full dress, a hundred thousand people crammed together, children hoisted on to shoulders, amid red balloons, hawkers selling coconuts and little paper flags.

Meanwhile Rue Chaptal dozed. The occasional cab went by, and now and again came the dull clip-clop of hooves on the wooden paving blocks.

At ten to four, Louis appeared. He had slipped a black jacket over his striped waistcoat and wore a black bowler hat. He stood framed in the entrance arch for a moment, lit a cigarette, blowing the smoke out defiantly, then he walked slowly to the corner of Rue Fontaine. Maigret watched him go into the tobacconist's.

He soon came out again and returned to the house. For a second, his gaze rested on the Vieux Calvados sign: it was too light outside and too dark inside for him to be able to recognize the secretary from the Saint-Georges police station.

Was he expecting someone? Was he trying to make up his mind? He walked to the corner of Rue Blanche and there he seemed to spot someone who was outside Maigret's field of vision. Then he hastened off and disappeared.

Maigret almost followed him. It was a sort of human respect that stopped him. He could feel the owner's bleary eyes on him. He would have to find an explanation, ask for the bill, wait for change, and then by the time he reached Rue Blanche, the butler would probably be far away.

He thought of another plan: calmly pay his bill and take advantage of Louis' absence to go and ring the doorbell of the house over the road, ask to speak to Mademoiselle Gendreau, or simply to young Marie.

On second thoughts, he did neither. A horse-drawn cab was approaching from Rue Blanche. The driver with the boiled leather hat carefully scrutinized the numbers on the houses and pulled up just past the Gendreau residence. He did not leave his seat. He seemed to have received orders. His meter flag was down.

Two or three minutes at most went by. Marie's mouse-like face appeared under the arch. She was still wearing her apron and lace cap. Then she vanished, came back with a travel bag, looked up and down the street and walked up to the cab.

Maigret couldn't hear what she said to the driver who, without leaving his perch, lifted up the bag, which couldn't have been heavy, and set it down beside him.

Marie returned to the house with a jaunty step. Her waist was as slender as that of the legendary Polaire's and she was so tiny that her mass of hair made her look as if she might overbalance.

She disappeared, and a moment later someone else appeared, a tall, curvaceous young woman wearing a navy-blue suit and a blue hat with a white veil decorated with large polka dots.

Why did Maigret turn red? Because he had seen her in her nightdress in a cluttered maid's room?

The woman was no maid, that was clear. She could only be Lise Gendreau. She walked over to the cab, very digni-fied despite her hurry, wiggling her hips a little, and clambered inside.

Maigret was so flustered that he almost forgot to make a note of the number of the cab: 48. He wrote it down straight away, and reddened again under Paumelle's stare.

'And there it is!' sighed the owner, wondering which jug to choose.

'There what is?'

'There's how it is with these so-called "good" families.'

He sounded jubilant, although he did not go so far as to smile.

'That's what you were waiting for, isn't it?'

'What do you mean?'

He became contemptuous and nudged a glass towards Maigret. Scowling, he appeared to be signalling: 'Since you are acting so secretively!'

And Maigret, to redeem himself, as if to curry the owner's favour:

'That's Mademoiselle Gendreau, isn't it?'

'Balthazar Coffee, yes, sir. And I don't think we'll be seeing her again in our street for a while.'

'Do you think she's gone travelling?'

The man's expression became crushing. He intimidated his young customer with the full weight of his fifty or sixty years, with all the little drinks he'd had with people of all kinds, with his knowledge of all the neighbourhood's secrets.

'Who are you working for?' he asked, suddenly cagey.

'But . . . I'm not working for anyone . . .'

A mere look, which said more bluntly than words: 'You're lying!'

Then, with a shrug:

'Too bad!'

'What did you think?'

'Go on, admit that you've already been sniffing around this area?'

'Me? I swear . . .'

It was true. He felt the need to prove his good faith. And the owner studied him calmly, seemed hesitant, and finally sighed:

'I had taken you for a friend of the count's.'

'What count?'

'It doesn't matter, since you aren't. You have the same walk at times, the same way of hunching your shoulders.'

'Do you think that Mademoiselle Gendreau went off to meet a count?'

Paumelle didn't reply as he had his eye on Louis, who had just reappeared at the corner of Rue Fontaine. Since setting off down Rue Blanche, he had walked around the block. He looked brighter than before. He really did appear to be out for a stroll, thinking of nothing other than enjoying the sunshine. He glanced up and down the empty street, then, like a man allowing himself a glass of well-earned white wine, he entered the tobacconist's on the corner.

'Does he sometimes come in here?'

A sharp, categorical '*No.*'

'He's an ugly-looking character.'

'There are a lot of ugly-looking people, but they can't do anything about it.'

Was he alluding to Maigret? He went on, as if talking to himself, while a clatter of crockery came from the kitchen:

'And there are some people who are honest and others who aren't.'

Maigret sensed that he was on the verge of an important revelation, but first he needed to win the trust of this heavy man drunk on calvados. Was it too late? He had probably not helped his cause by saying that he wasn't a friend of the count's. He had the distinct feeling that the entire morning had been fraught with misunderstandings.

'I work for a private detective agency,' he ventured on impulse.

'Well, well, well!'

Hadn't his boss told him not to bring the police into the case?

He was using deception to get to the truth. At that moment, he would have given a great deal to have been twenty years older and to have the owner's bulk and build.

'I knew something would happen.'

'And so it has, you see!'

'So you reckon she won't be coming back?'

He kept missing the mark, as Paumelle merely shrugged, not without a trace of pity. Then he tried another tactic.

'It's my round,' he announced, pointing to the earthenware flagons.

Would Paumelle refuse to drink with him? He shrugged again and muttered:

'At this hour, we'd do better to drink a bottle of cider.'

He went down to the cellar to fetch one. While Maigret felt groggy after all the calvados he had drunk, Paumelle still walked with a sure step and was unfazed by the staircase with no handrail, which was more like a ladder.

'You see, young man, you have to be an old dog in order to lie.'

'Do you think that I . . .'

Paumelle filled the glasses.

'Who would hire a private detective agency to deal with something like this? Not the count, right? Even less the Gendreau gentlemen, father or son. As for Monsieur Hubert . . .'

'Who's Hubert?'

'You see! You don't even know the family.'

'Is there another son?'

'How many houses are there in the street?'

'I don't know . . . Forty? . . . Fifty? . . .'

'Well, count them . . . Then, go and knock on every door. Perhaps you'll find someone who can tell you. In the meantime, excuse me, I'm not throwing you out. You can stay as long as you like, only it's time for my nap, and that's sacred.'

There was a straw-bottomed chair behind the bar, and Paumelle sat down in it, his back to the window, folded his hands over his belly, closed his eyes and appeared to fall asleep instantly.

Now that everything had gone quiet, his wife poked her head around the kitchen door, a tea-towel in one hand, a plate in the other, and, reassured, returned to her washing-up without a glance at Maigret, who sheepishly went over and sat by the window.

# 4. The Old Gentleman in Avenue du Bois

Maigret and Minard had agreed that when the latter returned from Conflans he would leave a note at Maigret's apartment on Boulevard Richard-Lenoir to let him know he was back.

'But it's out of your way!' Maigret had protested.

Minard's reply had been the usual:

'It doesn't matter.'

Maigret had asked him a question, tentatively, because he was loath to discourage the flautist.

'How are you going to introduce yourself? What do you intend to tell them?'

It was only now, with hindsight, as Maigret was walking home amid the bright lights of the boulevards after an exhausting day, that the musician's reply alarmed him somewhat.

'Don't worry, I'll think of something.'

But after a moment of gloom during the afternoon, perhaps because of the formidable owner of the Vieux Calvados, perhaps because he was having trouble digesting all the little glasses of calvados he'd drunk, Maigret now felt more cheerful.

Something was happening inside him which he had never experienced before. He couldn't have imagined that one day this sensation would become so familiar that it would become legendary at Quai des Orfèvres.

Up until that point it had only been a pleasant warmth pervading his body, a more confident stride and way of looking at people, shadows and lights, and at the cabs and trams all around him.

Earlier, in Rue Chaptal, he had resented his boss for allowing him to continue with this case and he half-suspected that Le Bret was deliberately playing a mean trick on him.

Can a man attack a fortress like the Balthazars' residence single-handed? Is that how the 'big boys' in the chief's squad worked? They had endless resources at their disposal – files, records, colleagues everywhere, informers. If they needed to have ten people followed, they put ten men on the job.

But now Maigret was suddenly happy to be working alone, snooping around as he pleased.

Neither did he foresee that one day he would be famous for this method, and that when he became head of the Crime Squad, with a small army of officers under his command, he would sometimes stake out a suspect in person, tail him in the street and sit in a café waiting for hours on end.

Before leaving the Vieux Calvados, where Paumelle was now showing him only the utmost indifference, he had made two more telephone calls. First of all to the Urbaine cab company, because Lise Gendreau's cab had borne its emblem. He was kept waiting for a long time.

'Number 48 belongs to the depot at La Villette. The cab

driver's name is Eugène Cornille. He went on duty at midday today. It's unlikely he'll be back at the depot before midnight.'

'You don't happen to know where I might find him in the meantime?'

'He usually waits at Place Saint-Augustin, but that of course depends on whether or not he picks up any customers. There's a little restaurant nearby called Au Rendez-vous du Massif Central. I believe he goes there for a bite to eat when he can.'

The other telephone call was to the vehicle registration department at the Préfecture. It took even longer to find the car registration number in the files. Since Maigret was supposedly calling from the police station, the clerk offered to call him back.

'I'd rather hold on.'

At long last he was given a name and an address: the Marquis de Bazancourt, 3, Avenue Gabriel.

Another affluent neighbourhood, probably a mansion overlooking the Champs-Élysées.

A haughty voice answered.

'Is it personal?'

And when he replied yes:

'Monsieur le marquis passed away three months ago.'

Then he asked a rather naive question:

'Does he have an heir?'

'I'm sorry? I don't understand. All his possessions have been sold, and only the house is still waiting for a buyer.'

'You don't know who purchased the De Dion-Bouton?'

'A mechanic from Rue des Acacias, off Avenue de la

Grande-Armée. I don't recall his name, but I think it's the only garage in the street.'

At five o'clock Maigret took the Métro to Étoile and found the garage in Rue des Acacias, but it was closed and there was a notice on the door saying:

*Please inquire next door.*

There was a shoe-mender on one side and a bar on the other. The notice meant people to inquire at the bar. Unfortunately, the wine merchant knew nothing.

'Dédé hasn't been in today. He does a bit of this and a bit of that, you know. Sometimes he goes on trips for his customers.'

'You wouldn't have his home address?'

'He lives in lodgings near Place des Ternes, but I don't know the exact address.'

'Is he married?'

Maigret couldn't be sure, because he didn't dare appear too inquisitive, but he had the sense that Dédé was a rather particular kind of gentleman and that, if he did have a companion, then he would be most likely to run into her in the street between Étoile and Place des Ternes.

He spent the rest of the afternoon trying to track down the cab driver, Cornille. He found Au Rendez-vous du Massif Central.

'It's rare for him not to drop in for a bite to eat.'

Annoyingly, today was one of those rare days. Not one of his fares had happened to finish up in the vicinity of Cornille's haunt in Place Saint-Augustin.

Maigret finally went home and walked under the archway. The concierge slid back the hatch in the glazed door.

'Monsieur Maigret! . . . Monsieur Maigret! . . . I have something important for you . . .'

It was a note which he was advised to read before going up to his apartment.

Don't go upstairs right away. I have to speak to you first. I waited as long as I could. Come and find me at the Brasserie Clichy. The young lady is upstairs, with your wife.

Your devoted servant,

Justin Minard.

By that time it was completely dark. Standing on the pavement, Maigret looked up, saw the curtains drawn in their apartment and pictured the two women in the little dining room that doubled as a sitting room. What on earth could they be talking about? Madame Maigret would most likely have laid the table, perhaps even served dinner.

He took the Métro to Place Blanche, and entered the vast brasserie where the air was thick with the smell of beer and sauerkraut. The little band of five musicians was playing. Justin wasn't playing the flute but the double bass. Dwarfed by the huge instrument, he looked even scrawnier.

Maigret sat down at one of the marble tables, couldn't make up his mind, and eventually ordered sauerkraut and a beer. When the piece was over, Minard joined him.

'I'm sorry to drag you all the way here, but I absolutely had to speak to you before you saw her.'

He was very agitated, perhaps a little worried, and that made Maigret anxious too.

'It hadn't occurred to me that her sister, being married, would have a different name from her. That made me lose time in my search for her. Her husband works for the railway, on the freight trains, and is often away for two or three days. They live in a house in the country, on a hillside, with a white goat tethered to a stake and a vegetable garden surrounded by a fence.'

'Was Germaine there?'

'When I arrived, the two of them were sitting at the table in front of a huge dish of black pudding and there was a strong smell of onions.'

'The sister hasn't given birth?'

'Not yet. They're waiting. Apparently it could still be a few more days. I told them I was an insurance salesman, that I'd heard that the young lady was about to have a baby and that it was the perfect time to take out a policy.'

The violinist, who was also the band leader, hung a card with a number on it from a rail, struck his rostrum with the tip of his bow, and Justin excused himself and went up on to the podium. When he came back, he said hurriedly:

'Don't worry. I'm sure everything will turn out fine. I'm quite well up on the subject because my wife has a bee in her bonnet about insurance. She claims I've only got about three years to live and that ... but it doesn't matter! Germaine is good-looking. She's plump, with a heavy chignon which she's always having to pin up again, and a penetrating gaze. You'll see! She stared at me continuously. She asked me point blank which company I worked for. I gave her a name off the top of my head, and then she wanted to know who my boss was. She fired a whole lot of questions at me and then she said: "I had a friend who worked in the same company for three months." Then, suddenly changing the subject, she asked, "Did Louis send you?"'

Justin Minard had to go back on stage. As the band struck up a Viennese waltz, he darted little glances at Maigret, as if to reassure him. He seemed to be saying: 'Don't worry, just wait for what's coming next!'

Next came:

'I told her that it wasn't Louis who'd sent me. "It's not the count, either!" she retorted. "No." "As for Monsieur Richard . . . Tell me, you wouldn't be one of Monsieur Richard's men, would you?" You see the type of girl? I had to make a decision. Her sister is younger than her and has been married for just a year. She was a housemaid in the Saint-Lazare neighbourhood, where she met her husband. Germaine rather enjoyed shocking her. If you want my opinion, she enjoys shocking people. She needs to be the centre of attention at any price, if you see what I mean.

'She probably dreamed of being an actress. After eating, she lit a cigarette, but she has no idea how to smoke.

'The house only has one room, with a big bed and an enlarged print of the wedding photo in an oval frame.

'"Are you sure you're not one of Monsieur Richard's men?" she asked me again.

'She has bulging eyes, and sometimes, when she's talking to you, she stares fixedly. It makes you squirm. It's as if all of a sudden she's no longer herself, but that's only an impression, because she's certainly got her head screwed

on. "You see how complicated life is in that world, Olga?"
she said to her sister indignantly. "I told you it would end
badly." I asked her when she planned to return to work.
"I don't think I'll ever set foot in that place again." And she
still wanted to know . . . So . . .'

Music! The flautist's eyes entreated Maigret to be
patient, not to worry.

'So there you are! Too bad if I did the wrong thing. I
told her the truth.'

'What truth?'

'That the young lady had called for help, that Louis had
hit me, that you had come and they'd shown you a girl in
a nightdress passing herself off as Germaine. That infuri-
ated her. I made it clear that there was no official
investigation, that you were handling the case in a private
capacity, that you'd be pleased to meet her and, before I'd
finished talking, she started to get dressed. I can still see
her in her lace-trimmed drawers and camisole, rummag-
ing in her suitcase, apologizing to her sister. "You do
understand," she said to her, "a baby always comes sooner
or later, whereas for me this is a matter of life or death."
I felt awkward, but I thought it would be useful for you to
hear it. I didn't know what to do with her. So I took her
to your place. I managed to have a word with your wife,
on the landing. My goodness! What a kind wife you have!
I told her not to let Germaine escape.

'Are you angry with me?'

How could he be angry? Maigret wasn't exactly reassured,
but all the same he sighed:

'Perhaps it's a good thing.'

'When will I see you?'

He remembered that he had to meet Cornille the cab driver at midnight.

'Maybe tonight.'

'If I don't see you, I'll take the liberty of dropping into your place tomorrow morning, now that I know where it is. Oh! One more thing . . .'

Embarrassed, he faltered:

'She asked me who would pay her expenses, and I told her . . . I didn't know what to say . . . I told her not to worry . . . But, you know, if it's a problem I . . .'

Maigret left while the band was playing and hurried towards the Métro. He felt a certain emotion on seeing the light under his door. He had no need to take his key out of his pocket because Madame Maigret always recognized his footsteps.

She gave him a knowing look, saying cheerfully:

'There's a charming young lady waiting for you.'

Dear Madame Maigret! She wasn't being sarcastic. She wanted to be hospitable. The creature was there, a dirty plate before her, elbows on the table, a cigarette in her mouth. Her huge eyes bored into Maigret as if she wanted to devour him. And yet there was still something hesitant about her.

'Are you really a policeman?'

He showed her his ID, and from then on she did not take her eyes off him. In front of her was a small glass: Madame Maigret had brought out the kirsch she kept for special occasions.

'I don't suppose you've eaten?'

'Yes, I have.'

'In that case, I'll leave you. I must do the washing-up.'

She cleared the table and went into the kitchen, not sure whether she should close the door.

'Is your friend a policeman too?'

'No. Not exactly. It was by chance . . .'

'Is he married?'

'Yes, I think so.'

He felt slightly uncomfortable in his own home, with this strange girl who was behaving as if this were her place, getting up, rearranging her chignon in front of the mirror on the chimney breast, then sitting down in Madame Maigret's armchair, muttering:

'May I?'

He asked her:

'Have you known Mademoiselle Gendreau long?'

'We were at school together.'

'I presume you are from Anseval, is that right? Did you both go to the school in Anseval?'

He was surprised that the Balthazar Coffee heiress had attended a little village school.

'I mean that we're the same age, give or take a couple of months. She'll be twenty-one next month, and I turned twenty-one a couple of weeks ago.'

'And you both went to school in Anseval?' he repeated.

'She didn't. She went to the convent in Nevers. But it was at the same time.'

He understood. And from then on he was cautious, taking care to separate the false from the true and the true from the partially true or the plausible.

'Were you expecting something to happen at Rue Chaptal?'

'I've always thought that things would turn nasty.'

'Why?'

'Because they hate one another.'

'Who?'

'Mademoiselle and her brother. I've worked at the house for four years. I started immediately after Madame's death. You know, don't you, that she died in a railway accident when she was on the way to take the waters at Vittel? It was terrible.'

She said that as if he had been present when they had recovered the hundred or so bodies from under the debris of the carriages.

'You see, while Madame was alive, the will wasn't important.'

'You know the family well.'

'I was born in Anseval. My father was born there. My grandfather was one of the count's farmers. He used to play marbles with the old gentleman when they were boys.'

'Which old gentleman?'

'That's how they still refer to him in the village. Don't you know anything? I thought the police knew everyone's business.'

'Presumably you're talking about old Monsieur Balthazar?'

'Monsieur Hector, yes. His father was the village saddler. He was also the church bell-ringer. At the age of twelve Monsieur Hector was a pedlar. He used to go from farm to farm with his box on his back.'

'Was it he who founded Balthazar Coffee?'

'Yes. Which didn't stop my grandfather being on familiar terms with him until the end. He didn't come back to the village for a very long time. When we saw him again, he was already rich, and we heard he'd bought the chateau.'

'Who had the chateau belonged to?'

'To the Count d'Anseval, of course.'

'And is there no longer a Count d'Anseval?'

'There is still one. Mademoiselle's friend. Won't you pour me another glass of liqueur? Is it from your region?'

'From my wife's.'

'When I think how that little shrew – I don't mean your wife – had the cheek to pretend she was me and sleep in my bed! Did you really see her in her nightdress? She's fatter than me. I could say a lot more about her body. Her breasts—'

'So, old Balthazar, the owner of Balthazar Coffee, bought the Château d'Anseval. Was he married?'

'He had been married, but his wife was already dead by then. He had a daughter, a beautiful woman, much too stuck-up. He also had a son, Monsieur Hubert, who's always been a good-for-nothing. He was as easy-going as his sister was tough. He travelled overseas a lot.'

'All that was before you were born?'

'Of course, but it's still going on!'

Maigret had automatically taken a notebook out of his pocket and was writing down names, rather as he would have drawn a family tree. He sensed that with a girl like Germaine it was important to get things straight.

'So, first of all there was Hector Balthazar, whom you call the old gentleman. When did he die?'

'Five years ago. Only one year before his daughter.'

And Maigret, thinking of Félicien Gendreau, who was elderly himself, said in surprise:

'He must have been very old?'

'He was eighty-eight. He lived alone in a huge house on Avenue du Bois-de-Boulogne. He still ran the business, with the help of his daughter.'

'Not his son?'

'You must be kidding! His son wasn't even allowed to set foot in the offices. He was given an allowance. He lives on the banks of the Seine, not far from Pont-Neuf. He's some sort of artist.'

'Just a minute . . . Avenue du Bois . . . Hector's daughter was married to Félicien Gendreau.'

'That's right. But Monsieur Félicien wasn't allowed to be involved in the business either.'

'Why not?'

'They tried, apparently, a long time ago . . . He was a gambler . . . Even now he spends his afternoons at the races . . . He's rumoured to have done something shady, with bank drafts, or cheques. His father-in-law wouldn't even speak to him any more.'

Later, Maigret would become acquainted with the mansion on Avenue du Bois-de-Boulogne, one of the ugliest, most pretentious houses in Paris, with medieval turrets and stained-glass windows. He would also see a photograph of the old man, with his chiselled features, chalky complexion and long white side whiskers, wearing a frock coat open to reveal two slim strips of shirt-front either side of his black cravat.

If he had been better acquainted with Paris life, he would have known that the elderly Balthazar had bequeathed his mansion to the state, with his entire collection of paintings, on condition that it be turned into a museum. The newspapers had been full of it when he died. For over a year, the experts had argued, and the government had ended up refusing the legacy, having discovered that most of the paintings were forgeries.

One day Maigret would see the portrait of the daughter too, her hair drawn back at the nape, reminiscent of Empress Eugénie, her face as cold as that of the founder of the Balthazar dynasty.

As for Félicien Gendreau, he had met him, with his dyed moustache, light-coloured spats and his cane with its gold knob.

'Apparently the old man hated everyone, including his son, then his son-in-law, and finally Monsieur Richard, whom he knew well. The only exceptions were his daughter and his granddaughter, Mademoiselle Lise. He used to say that they alone were of his stock, and he left a complicated will. Monsieur Braquement would be able to tell you about it.'

'Who is Monsieur Braquement?'

'His lawyer. He's in his eighties. All the others are afraid of him, because he's the only person who knows.'

'Who knows what?'

'I was never told. All will be revealed when Mademoiselle Lise turns twenty-one, and that's why they're all so worked up at the moment. As for me, I don't take any sides . . . If I'd wanted to . . .'

He had a sudden hunch.

'Monsieur Richard?' he asked, egging her on.

'He was always after me. I told him that he was barking up the wrong tree and that he'd do better to go after Marie. "She's stupid enough to fall for your nonsense," I said to his face.'

'Did he take your advice?'

'I have no idea. With those people, you never can tell. As far as I'm concerned – and I know them well! – they're all a bit crazy.'

As she said this, her eyes bulged more than ever, and her fixed stare was disconcerting. She leaned towards Maigret as if about to grab his knees.

'Is Louis also from Anseval?'

'He's the son of the former schoolmaster. Some people say that he's actually the priest's son.'

'Is he on Monsieur Richard's side?'

'What are you saying? Quite the opposite, he spends his life running around after Mademoiselle. He stayed with the old man until his death. He's the one who cared for him during his illness and he probably knows more than anyone else, perhaps even more than Monsieur Braquement.'

'He never made a pass at you?'

'Him?'

She hooted.

'He'd have a hard job! He looks like a man, with all that black hair. But first of all he's much older than people think. He's at least fifty-five. And he's not a real man, if you understand my meaning. That's why Madame Louis and Albert—'

'Sorry. Who is Albert?'

'The manservant. He comes from Anseval too. He was a jockey until he was twenty-one.'

'Excuse me. I was shown around the entire house, but I didn't see a bedroom that—'

'Because he sleeps above the stables, with Jérôme.'

'Jérôme?'

'Monsieur Félicien's coachman. Arsène, the chauffeur, is the only one who doesn't sleep in the house because he's married and has a child.'

Maigret had scribbled down the names higgledy-piggledy in his notebook.

'If someone shot Mademoiselle, and that wouldn't surprise me, it's bound to be Monsieur Richard, during one of their arguments.'

'Do they often argue?'

'Pretty much every day. Once, he grabbed her wrists so hard that she had two blue rings around them for a week. But she fights back, and she's given him some vicious kicks to his legs and even a bit higher. But I'll bet that the shot wasn't aimed at Mademoiselle.'

'Who was it aimed at, then?'

'At the count!'

'What count?'

'Don't you understand anything? The Count d'Anseval.'

'Really! There's still a Count d'Anseval.'

'The grandson of the one who sold the chateau to old

Balthazar. It's Mademoiselle who found him, I've no idea where.'

'Is he wealthy?'

'Him? He hasn't got a bean.'

'And he's a visitor to the house?'

'He visits Mademoiselle.'

'He . . . I mean . . .'

'Are you asking me if he sleeps with her? I don't think he wants to. Now do you understand? They're all barmy. They fight like dogs. Monsieur Hubert's the only one who minds his own business, but the other two – the brother and the sister – try to drag him into things.'

'Are you talking about Hubert Balthazar, the old man's son? How old is he?'

'Fifty, maybe? Perhaps a bit older? He's very elegant, very distinguished. When he comes, he always stops and has a chat with me. Oh goodness! It's so late, there are no more trains for Conflans and I have to sleep somewhere. Do you have a bed here?'

There was something so provocative in her eyes that Maigret cleared his throat and glanced instinctively towards the kitchen door.

'I'm afraid we don't have a spare room. We've only just moved in.'

'Are you newlyweds?'

In her mouth, the word sounded almost lewd.

'I'll find you a room in a nearby hotel.'

'Are you going to bed already?'

'I have another appointment in town.'

'It's true that you police officers probably don't sleep in

your own beds that often. It's funny, you don't look one bit like a policeman. I once knew one, a local policeman, tall, very dark-haired, Léonard . . .'

Maigret didn't want to hear about Léonard. She seemed to have known a lot of men, including the insurance agent.

'I expect you'll be needing me again? The best way would be for me to go back to their place, as if nothing were amiss. And then I could report to you every evening.'

A clatter of saucepans came from the kitchen, but that was not why Maigret declined Germaine's offer. She literally terrified him.

'I'll see you tomorrow. If you'd like to come with me . . .'

Before putting on her hat and coat, she rearranged her hair again in front of the mirror and grabbed the bottle of kirsch:

'May I? I've talked so much, thought so much! Aren't you drinking?'

There was no point telling her how many small glasses of calvados he'd downed earlier in the day, willingly or not.

'I'm sure I've got lots more to tell you. There are people who write novels who haven't experienced a fraction of the things I have. Now if I were to start writing . . .'

He went into the kitchen and kissed his wife on the forehead. She gave him a cheerful look, with a mischievous twinkle in her eyes.

'I may not be back until fairly late.'

And she teased:

'Take your time, Jules!'

There was a lodging house just before Boulevard Voltaire. In the street, Germaine deliberately grabbed hold of her companion's arm.

'It's my Louis heels . . .'

Indeed! She was more used to wearing clogs!

'I think your wife's very nice. She's a very good cook.'

He didn't dare give her the money for her room. He went into the office and blushed when the night-duty clerk asked him:

'Is it for the night or for a couple of hours?'

'For the night. Just for the lady.'

While the clerk looked at his key board, Germaine leaned even more heavily on Maigret's arm, with no excuse now that she wasn't walking.

'Number 18. Second floor on the left. Wait and I'll fetch you some towels.'

Maigret would rather forget how he took leave of her. There was a strip of red carpet on the stairs. She was holding her two towels in one hand, and her key dangling from a copper tag in the other. The clerk had gone back to reading his newspaper.

'Are you sure you don't have any more questions for me?'

She stood on the first stair. Her eyes were bulging, staring more intently than ever. What was it about her that reminded him of the praying mantis which devours the male after mating?

'No . . . Not today . . .' he must have stuttered.

'I was forgetting that you had an appointment.'

Her moist lips curled in a mocking smile.

'So, see you tomorrow?'

'Tomorrow, yes.'

At least that is how it must have gone. Maigret wasn't used to such things yet. He only recalled the smell of fresh laundry as he raced down the steps to the Métro, the click of the automatic turnstiles, a long ride in the subterranean greyness, with human shapes swaying with each jolt of the train, glazed eyes, faces gnawed by shadow under the wan electric lights.

He lost his way in the ill-lit, empty streets around Porte de La Villette. Eventually he came across a vast open depot, cluttered with stationary carriages, shafts pointing upwards, and behind it, on the other side of a courtyard, the warmth of stables.

'Cornille? No, he's not back yet. Do you want to wait for him?'

It wasn't until half past midnight that a completely drunk cab driver looked at him in amazement.

'The little lady from Rue Chaptal? Hold on! She was the one who gave me a one-franc tip. And the tall, dark-haired fellow.'

'What tall, dark-haired fellow?'

'I mean the one who hailed me in Rue Blanche and told me to go and wait in Rue Chaptal opposite number . . . number . . . That's funny, I can never remember numbers . . . even though in my job—'

'Did you drive her to the station?'

'To the station? Which station?'

His eyes were swimming, and the juice from the tobacco

he was chewing nearly landed on Maigret's trousers when he spat it out in a long stream.

'First of all, it wasn't to the station . . . And then . . . Then it must have been . . .'

Maigret slipped him a franc.

'It was to the hotel opposite the Tuileries, in a little square . . . Hold on. It's named after a monument . . . I always muddle up the names of monuments . . . The Hôtel du Louvre . . . Gee up . . .'

There were no more Métros, or omnibuses, or trams, and Maigret had to walk back down the interminable Rue de Flandre before he reached the bright lights of a livelier neighbourhood.

The Brasserie Clichy would be closed by now, and Justin Minard had probably gone home to his apartment in Rue d'Enghien, where he would be giving an account of himself to his wife.

## 5. Maigret's Earliest Ambition

Maigret was shaving in front of his mirror, which he had hooked over the window catch in the dining room. He was in the habit of following his wife around the apartment every morning, washing and shaving in whichever room she happened to be in, perhaps because it was their best moment together. Madame Maigret had one particularly pleasing quality: she was as fresh and cheerful on waking as she was in the middle of the afternoon. They opened the windows and breathed in the morning air. They could hear hammering from a smithy, the rumble of lorries, horses whinnying, and they even caught warm whiffs of manure when the stables of the removals company next door were being cleaned out.

'Do you think she really is mad?'

'If she'd stayed in her village, got married and had ten children, probably no one would have noticed. They might not all have been from the same father, that's all.'

'Look! Isn't that your friend pacing up and down the street?'

He leaned out, one cheek covered in lather, and spotted Justin Minard waiting patiently for him.

'Aren't you going to invite him up?'

'There's no point. I'll be ready in five minutes. Were you planning to go out today?'

Maigret rarely inquired about her plans, and she guessed at once.

'Do you want me to chaperone the young lady?'

'It's highly likely that I will ask you. I can't let her loose in Paris, given that she simply can't keep her mouth shut. Goodness knows who she'll speak to or what she'll tell them.'

'Are you going to see her now?'

'Right away.'

'She'll still be in bed.'

'Probably.'

'I bet you'll have a job getting away from her.'

As he emerged from under the arch Minard stopped him and began to walk alongside him, completely at ease, asking:

'What are we doing today, chief?'

Years later, Maigret would remember that the little flautist had been the first person to call him chief.

'Did you see her? Do you have any leads? I hardly slept. Just as I was about to doze off, a question came into my mind.'

Their footsteps echoed on the pavement of Boulevard Richard-Lenoir. From a distance they could see the crowds on Boulevard Voltaire.

'If a shot was fired, it must have been aimed at someone. So I was wondering whether it had hit home. Am I boring you?'

On the contrary, since the same question had occurred to Maigret.

'Supposing the shot didn't hit anyone. Of course it's difficult to imagine yourself in the shoes of people like that . . . But it seems to me that if no one was wounded or killed, they wouldn't have put on such an elaborate performance . . . Do you follow me? . . . As soon as they'd thrown me out, they hurriedly tidied the room to make it look as if no one had set foot inside . . . There's another detail: do you remember, while the butler was trying to get rid of me, a voice from the landing said: "Hurry up, Louis!", as if there was some trouble up there. And, if they had to stick the young lady in the maid's room, it's probably because she was too upset to play her part . . .

'I'm free all day . . . You can send me anywhere you like . . .'

Next to the lodging house where Germaine had spent the night there was a café with a terrace, pedestal tables with white marble tops, a waiter with side whiskers straight out of a promotional calendar who was cleaning the windows with whiting.

'Wait here for me.'

He had hesitated. He had almost sent Minard upstairs in his place. Had anyone asked him why he needed to see Germaine, he would have found it hard to reply. That morning, he wished he could be in several places at once. He was feeling almost nostalgic for the Vieux Calvados and was sorry not to be sitting by the window watching the comings and goings of the house in Rue Chaptal. Now that he was better acquainted with all the people who lived there, it seemed to him that the sight of Richard Gendreau getting into his motor-car, or his father walking towards his carriage, or Louis coming out into the street for a breath of air would have a precise significance.

He also wished he could be at the Hôtel du Louvre, Avenue du Bois, or even in Anseval.

But only one of these characters – all of them unknown to him two days earlier – was accessible to him, and he instinctively clung to him.

Curiously, that feeling was rooted in the dreams of his childhood and adolescent years. His father's premature death had put an end to his medical studies after two years, but the fact was that he had never intended to become a real doctor treating patients.

The profession he had always yearned for did not actually exist. As he grew up, he had the sense that many people in his village were out of place, that they had followed a path that was not theirs, purely because they didn't know what else to do.

And he imagined a very clever, above all very understanding man, a cross between a doctor and a priest, a man capable of understanding another's destiny at first glance.

His reply to his wife on the subject of Germaine fitted that image: if she'd stayed in Anseval . . .

People would have come to see him the way they consulted a doctor. He would have been a sort of mender of destinies. Not only because he was clever. Perhaps he didn't need to have an exceptional mind but simply to be able to live the life of every man, to put himself in anyone's shoes.

Maigret had never spoken of this to a soul; he didn't dare think about it too much, because he would have laughed at himself. Prevented from completing his medical studies, he had joined the police by chance. But was it really chance? And aren't the police sometimes menders of destinies?

He had spent the entire night, sometimes awake, sometimes asleep, among those people whom he barely knew, starting with the elderly Balthazar who had died five years earlier. Now, as he knocked on Germaine's door, he had the entire clan with him.

'Come in!' replied a husky voice.

Then, immediately after:

'Hold on! I forgot the door's locked.'

She was barefoot in her nightdress, her hair cascading down her back, her plump breasts heaving with vitality. But she had clearly been awake for a while, because on the bedside table was a tray with some left-over hot chocolate and croissant crumbs.

'Are we going out? Do I need to get dressed?'

'You can either get back into bed or put on some clothes. I simply want to have a chat with you.'

'Don't you feel awkward standing there fully clothed while I'm in my nightdress?'

'No.'

'Doesn't your wife get jealous?'

'No. I'd like you to talk to me about Count d'Anseval. Or rather . . . you know the house, the people who live in it and the regular visitors . . . Imagine that it's one o'clock in the morning . . . One o'clock in the morning . . . An argument breaks out in Mademoiselle Gendreau's room . . . Think hard . . . Who, in your opinion, might be in her room?'

She had started to comb her hair in front of the mirror,

displaying the auburn tufts under her arms, her rosy flesh visible through her nightdress. She racked her brains.

'Louis?' he prompted.

'No. Louis wouldn't have gone upstairs so late.'

'Wait a minute. There's a detail I forgot to mention. Louis was fully dressed, with his tailcoat, his starched white shirt-front and his black tie. Does he generally go to bed late?'

'Sometimes, but he doesn't keep his butler's uniform on. That means there was a visitor in the house.'

'Could Hubert Balthazar, Mademoiselle Gendreau's uncle, have been in his niece's bedroom, for example?'

'I don't think he'd have come at one o'clock in the morning.'

'If he had, where would she have entertained him? In one of the downstairs drawing rooms, I imagine?'

'Definitely not. That's not how they do things in Rue Chaptal. They all lead separate lives. The drawing rooms are only for receptions. The rest of the time, they all stay shut away in their own rooms.'

'Could Richard Gendreau have gone up to his sister's room?'

'Definitely. He often did. Especially when he was angry.'

'Did he sometimes carry a pistol? Have you ever seen him with a gun in his hand?'

'No.'

'What about Mademoiselle Gendreau?'

'Just a minute! Monsieur Richard owns two guns, a big one and a little one, but they are in his desk. Mademoiselle has one too, with a mother-of-pearl grip. She keeps it in her bedside table drawer. Every night, she takes it out and puts it on the table.'

'Is she afraid?'

'No. She's wary. Like all shrews, she always reckons someone's got it in for her. Supposing I told you that she's already a miser, even at her age. She leaves small change lying around on purpose, having counted it, to see if anyone will steal a few sous. The maid before Marie got caught and was fired.'

'Has she ever entertained the count in her bedroom?'

'Maybe not exactly in her bedroom, but in the boudoir next door.'

'At one o'clock in the morning?'

'Probably. I read a book about that English queen, Elizabeth I . . . Have you heard of her? I know it's a novel, but it must be true . . . She was a cold woman, who couldn't make love. I wouldn't be surprised if Mademoiselle was like that too.'

The comb rasped through her hair and she arched her back, glancing occasionally at Maigret in the mirror.

'I'm glad I'm not like that!'

'Is it possible that, on hearing a noise coming from the second floor, Monsieur Richard could have rushed upstairs with his pistol?'

She shrugged.

'What for?'

'To catch his sister's lover . . .'

'That wouldn't bother him. The only thing those people care about is money.'

She continued to flaunt herself in front of him, oblivious

of the fact that he was miles away, his thoughts on the bedroom in Rue Chaptal, trying to position all the main actors, like a theatre director.

'Has Count d'Anseval ever brought a friend with him?'

'It's possible, but then she would have entertained him downstairs, and I hardly ever went down.'

'Did Mademoiselle Lise telephone him sometimes?'

'I don't think he has a telephone. She didn't call him; now and then he called her, probably from a café.'

'How did she address him?'

'Jacques, of course.'

'How old is he?'

'Twenty-five, perhaps? He's a handsome fellow, but there's something thuggish about him. He always looks as if he's making fun of people.'

'Is he the sort of man who'd carry a gun in his pocket?'

'Definitely.'

'Why are you so sure?'

'Because he's that sort of fellow. Have you read the *Fantômas* books?'

'Monsieur Félicien, the father, does he side with his daughter or with his son?'

'He doesn't side with anyone. Or rather, he's on my side, if you really want to know. He sometimes shuffles into my room in his slippers at eight in the morning, saying he needs a button sewing on.

'The others pretty much ignore him. The servants call him the old boy, or mutton chops. Apart from Albert, who's his personal manservant, no one takes any notice of what he says. They know it's of no importance. Once,

I said to him bluntly: "If you keep getting all excited like this, you'll have a heart attack. And that won't do you any good!" That didn't stop him. Now it's Marie's turn, and I don't know whether she gave in . . .

'By the way, aren't you embarrassed watching a woman getting dressed?'

Maigret rose and looked for his hat.

'Where are you off to? You're not going to leave me all on my own?'

'I have some important meetings to attend. In a moment, my friend who brought you here will come and keep you company.'

'Where is he?'

'Downstairs.'

'Why didn't you bring him up? Admit that you had something in mind! Are you scared? Because of your wife?'

She had already poured water into the bowl to wash, and Maigret could see she was about to slip off her night-dress, the straps of which slid down a little further every time she moved.

'I'll probably see you at some point during the day,' he said, opening the door.

He found Justin Minard enjoying a café-crème on the terrace of the café, illuminated by a slanting ray of sunshine.

'Your wife was here a moment ago.'

'What?'

'Just after you left, an urgent letter arrived. She ran to try and catch up with you. When I saw her, I realized that she was looking for you.'

Maigret sat down, ordered a beer without thinking, oblivious of the time of day, and opened the letter delivered by pneumatic tube. It was signed Maxime Le Bret.

*I should like you to come into the office this morning. Regards.*

It had definitely been written from his home on Boulevard de Courcelles because if he had sent it from the office, Le Bret would have used headed notepaper. He was a stickler for etiquette. He had at least four different visiting cards for different purposes: *Monsieur and Madame Le Bret de Plouhinec*, *Maxime Le Bret de Plouhinec*, *Maxime Le Bret, Officer of the Legion of Honour*, *Maxime Le Bret, Detective Chief Inspector*.

This handwritten note marked a new intimacy between him and his secretary, and he must have thought carefully about how to begin: Dearest Maigret? Dear Jules? Monsieur? In the end, he had resolved the problem by putting nothing.

'Tell me, Minard, do you really have some time on your hands?'

'As much time as you need.'

'The young lady is upstairs. I don't know when I'll be free. I'm worried that if we allow her to wander around on her own, she might go to Rue Chaptal and blab.'

'I understand.'

'If you go out with her, leave me a note telling me where you are. If you need to get away, leave her with my wife.'

A quarter of an hour later, Maigret walked into the police station and his colleagues looked at him with that slightly envious admiration reserved for officers on leave or on a special mission — those lucky enough to escape the daily grind.

'Has the chief inspector arrived?'

'Ages ago.'

There was the same hint of friendliness in Le Bret's voice as in his note. He even proffered his hand, which he did not usually do.

'I shan't ask you how your investigation is progressing, as I imagine it's still early days. I asked you to come and see me . . . I'd like to make one thing clear, because this is a delicate matter. Although anything I find out when I'm at home in Boulevard de Courcelles is certainly no business of the chief inspector, on the other hand . . .'

He paced up and down the office, his face fresh and rested, puffing on his gold-tipped cigarette.

'I don't want to leave you to stew for want of a piece of information. Yesterday evening Mademoiselle Gendreau telephoned my wife.'

'Did she telephone from the Hôtel du Louvre?'

'You know?'

'She took a cab there in the afternoon.'

'In that case . . . That's all . . . I'm aware of how hard it is to find out what goes on in some houses.'

He sounded anxious, as if he was wondering what else Maigret might have discovered.

'She has no intention of returning to Rue Chaptal and she plans to restore her grandfather's house.'

'Avenue du Bois-de-Boulogne.'

'Yes. I see that you already know a great deal.'

Emboldened, Maigret asked:

'May I take the liberty of asking whether you know Count d'Anseval?'

Surprised, Le Bret frowned, as if trying to understand. He racked his brains for a moment.

'Oh! Yes. The Balthazars bought the Chateau d'Anseval. That's right, isn't it? But I don't see the connection.'

'Mademoiselle Gendreau and Count d'Anseval used to meet each other regularly.'

'Are you sure? That's rather strange.'

'Do you know the count?'

'Not personally, and I'd prefer not to. But I have heard about him. What I find surprising . . . Unless they're old childhood friends, or she's not aware . . . Bob d'Anseval has gone off the rails. All doors are closed to him, he's not a member of any club, and I think he's been in trouble with the Drug Squad on several occasions.'

'Do you happen to have his address?'

'He's said to hang around certain disreputable little bars in Avenue de Wagram and around Place des Ternes. Perhaps the Drug Squad will be able to help.'

'May I ask them?'

'On condition you don't mention the Gendreau-Balthazars.'

He was visibly anxious. He muttered to himself a couple of times:

'How strange!'

And, bolder still, Maigret asked:

'Do you think that Mademoiselle Gendreau is a normal person?'

This time, Le Bret gave a start and shot his secretary an unintentionally stern look.

'Pardon?'

'I'm sorry if I phrased my question awkwardly. I'm convinced that it was Lise Gendreau I saw in the maid's room on the night in question. Which means that something had happened in her room that was serious enough to require a cover-up, and I have no reason to doubt the testimony of the musician who heard a gunshot as he was walking down the street.'

'Go on.'

'It is probable that Mademoiselle Gendreau was not alone with her brother in her room that night.'

'What are you saying?'

'That, in all likelihood, the third person was Count d'Anseval. If a shot was fired, if there really were three people in the room, if one of them was hit . . .'

Maigret glowed inwardly at Le Bret's astonished expression.

'Have you found out anything else?'

'Not a lot.'

'I thought you were shown around the entire house.'

'Apart from the bedrooms above the stables and the garage.'

For a moment, and for the first time, the drama took on substance. Le Bret had accepted the possibility that a violent event had taken place – a murder, or an assault. And it had taken place in his world, among people who belonged to his social circle, people he met at his club, in the room of a young lady who was a close friend of his own wife.

It was strange to see his boss flummoxed, and Maigret was aware of the tension. No longer was there simply a problem to be resolved, but there was a human life, perhaps several human lives, at stake.

'Mademoiselle Gendreau is very wealthy,' sighed Le Bret at length, with regret. 'She is probably the sole heiress to one of the five or six biggest fortunes in Paris.'

'Probably?'

His superior knew more than he was letting on, but his society-gentleman self was clearly struggling to come to the aid of his chief-inspector self.

'You see, Maigret, there are huge interests at stake, and Lise Gendreau has known all her life that she is at the centre of these. She never was an ordinary little girl. She always knew she was the Balthazar Coffee heiress, and furthermore that she was Hector Balthazar's spiritual heiress.'

He added wistfully:

'Poor girl.'

Then, becoming alert:

'Are you certain of what you told me about d'Anseval?'

It was Le Bret the man of the world who was intrigued by this question and who, despite everything, was still incredulous.

'He would often visit Mademoiselle Gendreau late at night, if not in her bedroom, then in her boudoir on the second floor.'

'That's different.'

Was this distinction between the boudoir and the bedroom enough to reassure him?

'I'd like to ask you another question, if I may, sir. Has Mademoiselle Gendreau ever intended to marry? Is she interested in men? Do you think she might be what's described as "frigid"?'

Le Bret couldn't believe his ears. He stared dumbstruck at his young secretary who had suddenly come out with such language, moreover in connection with people he'd never even met. Le Bret's expression was a mixture of reluctant admiration and slight concern, as if he had unexpectedly come face to face with a wizard.

'There's a lot of gossip about her. She has certainly turned down the most dazzling offers.'

'Is she reputed to have lovers?'

The chief inspector was obviously lying when he replied:

'I don't know.'

Then he added sharply:

'I confess that I don't take the liberty of speculating on such matters where my wife's friends are concerned. You see, my young friend . . .'

He was almost brusque, as he probably would have been had they been at his home on Boulevard de Courcelles, but he checked himself in time.

'. . . our profession requires extreme caution and tact. I even wonder . . .'

Maigret felt a shiver run down his spine. He was going to be told to drop the case and to go back to being a pen-pusher at his black desk, copying statements into registers and writing out certificates of hardship.

For a few seconds, the sentence hung in the air.

Fortunately, the police chief gained the upper hand over the society gentleman.

'Listen to me: be very, very careful. If you run into any trouble, telephone me at home if necessary. I think I've already said that to you. Do you have my number?'

He wrote it down on a scrap of paper.

'I asked you to come and see me this morning because I didn't want to leave you floundering. I had no idea that you'd already made such good progress.'

However, he did not extend his hand. Maigret had become a police officer again, and a police officer who was about to bumble into a world where the visiting card *Monsieur and Madame Le Bret de Plouhinec* alone had currency.


Maigret walked through the arch of Quai des Orfèvres just before midday. He passed the room whose walls were plastered with criminal record cards. He climbed up the wide, dusty staircase, not as the bearer of a message from the police station but in pursuit of his own ends.

He took in the doors along the corridor with the names of the detective chief inspectors on them, the glassed-in waiting room, an inspector who walked past escorting a man in handcuffs.

Now he was in an office whose open windows overlooked the Seine, an office that was a far cry from that of his neighbourhood police station. Men were sitting in front of telephones or report sheets; an inspector, one leg resting on his desk, was calmly smoking his pipe; the place was alive, buzzing, the atmosphere one of relaxed camaraderie.

'Look, kid, you can always try going up to "Records" to see if there's a file on him, but I don't think there is, because he has never been sentenced, as far as I know.'

A sergeant in his forties treated him affably, as if he were a choirboy. This was the Drug Squad. These people knew Count d'Anseval's milieu inside out.

'Tell me, Vanel, how long is it since you've seen the count?'

'Bob?'

'Yes.'

'The last time I bumped into him was at the races, and he was with Dédé.'

They explained:

'Dédé's the fellow who has a garage in Rue des Acacias. A garage where there are never more than one or two cars. Get it, kid?'

'Cocaine?'

'Most likely. And probably other little rackets on the side. Not to mention the women. The Count, as he's called, is in it up to his neck. We could have picked him up for a couple of minor offences, but we prefer to keep an eye on him in the hope that eventually he'll lead us to bigger fish.'

'Do you have his most recent address?'

'Don't you think your boss is treading on our toes? Watch it, kid! Don't put the wind up Bob. Not that we have any particular interest in him, but a depraved fellow like him can often be very useful to us. Is this case of yours a big one?'

'I really need to find him.'

'Have you got the address, Vanel?'

And a surly Vanel, with the contempt of those at Quai des Orfèvres for lowly local police officers, said:

'Hôtel du Centre, Rue Brey. Just behind Étoile.'

'When was he last there?'

'Four days ago, I saw him at the café on the corner of Rue Brey with his tart.'

'May I ask her name?'

'Lucile. She's easy to spot. She has a scar on her left cheek.'

A harassed inspector came in with a bundle of papers in his hand.

'Tell me, boys—'

He stopped at the sight of an outsider in his inspectors' office and looked inquiringly at his men.

'The secretary from the Saint-Georges station.'

'Ah!'

And that 'ah!' made Maigret long all the more fervently to be one of the 'boys' at Quai des Orfèvres. He was a nobody! Less than a nobody! No one paid him any further attention. Leaning towards the sergeant, the chief inspector was discussing a raid planned for the following night in the vicinity of Rue de La Roquette.

Since he wasn't far from République, he decided to go home for lunch before going to the Étoile neighbourhood in search of the count or Lucile.

He was about to turn into Boulevard Richard-Lenoir when he spotted a couple in the brasserie sitting at a table set for two.

It was Justin Minard and Germaine. He had to hurry

past, to avoid being waylaid by them. He had the feeling that the flautist had seen him and was pretending to look elsewhere. But Mademoiselle Gendreau's maid tapped on the window and he had no option but to go inside.

'I was worried you'd go to the lodging house and find no one there,' said Germaine. 'Have you been very busy?'

Minard looked shamefaced as he scrutinized the menu.

Germaine, on the other hand, was radiant. Her skin looked clearer, her cheeks pinker, her eyes brighter, and even her breasts were fuller.

'Do you need us this afternoon? Because, if you don't, I saw there's a matinée at the Théâtre de l'Ambigu . . .'

They were both sitting on the imitation leather banquette, and Maigret noticed Germaine's hand resting on the musician's knee with a calm assurance.

The two men's eyes eventually met. The flautist's said: 'I had no choice.'

And Maigret forced himself to keep a straight face.

He was going to have a cosy lunch with Madame Maigret, in their little dining room on the fourth floor from where they had a foreshortened view of the passers-by in the street.

Madame Maigret suddenly blurted out, while they were in the middle of talking about something else:

'I bet she had him!' without suspecting for a moment that the buxom girl might have had her husband too.

# 6. A Little Family Party

It wasn't until eight o'clock that evening, when it was dark and the avenues radiating from the Arc de Triomphe were outlined by the pearly glow from the gas lamps, that Maigret, who was beginning to lose hope, finally found what he was looking for.

He had a golden memory of his afternoon, Paris at its most beautiful, the spring air so mild and fragrant that people stopped to inhale it. Women had probably been going out without a jacket during the warmest hours for the past few days, but it was only now that he noticed. He felt as if he were witnessing a blossoming of flimsy dresses, and there were already daisies, poppies and cornflowers on their hats, while the men ventured out in boaters.

That afternoon he had combed a narrow sector between Étoile, Place des Ternes and Porte Maillot for hours on end. On turning the corner into Rue Brey, he ran into three tightly corseted women teetering in high-heeled boots who were not talking or standing together but would rush over as soon as a passing man appeared. Their home base was the hotel where the count lived. Just inside the doorway stood another woman, much fatter and more placid than the others, not bothering to cast her net wide.

Why was Maigret struck by the laundry opposite, where

fresh-faced girls were ironing? Was it because of the contrast?

'Is the count upstairs?' he asked at the desk.

The receptionist looked him up and down. The people he was to meet that day would all have the same way of sizing him up, as if in slow motion, looking bored rather than contemptuous. The reluctant answer came:

'Go up and see.'

He believed he had already cleared the first hurdle.

'Can you tell me his room number?'

A hesitation. He had just let slip that he was not one of the count's friends.

'Thirty-two . . .'

He went up the stairs, where the smell of human life and cooking hung in the air. At the far end of the corridor, a chambermaid was collecting up bed sheets which still seemed damp with sweat. He knocked at a door in vain.

'Is it to see Lucile?' asked the maid from a distance.

'No, the count.'

'He's not there. No one's in.'

'Do you happen to know where I might find him?'

The question must have sounded so ridiculous that she didn't take the trouble to reply.

'What about Lucile?'

'Isn't she at Le Coq?'

There again he had given himself away, instantly arousing suspicion. If he didn't even know where to find Lucile, what was he doing there?

Le Coq was one of the two cafés on the corner of Avenue de Wagram with a wide terrace. A few lone women were sitting at tables, and Maigret suspected there was a slight difference between them and the women soliciting on the corner of Rue Brey. There was yet another type, the women who walked slowly up to Étoile, then back down again to Place des Ternes, pausing to look in the shop windows. Some of them could have been mistaken for wealthy women out for a stroll.

Maigret looked for a girl with a scar. He spoke to the waiter.

'Is Lucile not here?'

A quick glance around the room.

'I haven't seen her today.'

'Do you think she'll be coming? Have you not seen the count either?'

'He hasn't been in for at least three days.'

He reached Rue des Acacias. The garage was still closed. The shoe-mender, chewing tobacco, also seemed to find Maigret's questions pointless.

'I think I saw him take the car out this morning.'

'A grey car? A De Dion-Bouton?'

For the man chewing quid, a car was a car and he paid no attention to the model.

'You don't happen to know where I might find him?'

And the man sitting in his gloomy shop looked at him with something bordering on pity.

'I just mend shoes . . .'

Maigret returned to Rue Brey, went upstairs and knocked at number 32, but there was no reply. For over an hour he continued his search, from Le Coq to Place des Ternes, turning his head to stare at every woman, looking for a face with a scar. They thought he was a punter who couldn't make up his mind.

He felt the occasional twinge of anguish and berated himself for wasting his time, when something more important might be happening elsewhere. He had promised himself, if he had the leisure, to go and sniff around the offices of Balthazar Coffee, check whether Lise Gendreau was still at the Hôtel du Louvre, and he would also like to have kept an eye on the comings and goings in Rue Chaptal.

Why did he persist? He saw solemn-looking men enter the hotel in Rue Brey with their heads lowered, as if they were being pulled by an invisible leash. He saw men come out, even more shamefaced, their expressions anxious, who quickly strode over the empty space between them and the crowd, regaining their confidence as they melted into it. He saw women signalling to each other, sharing out silver coins.

He went into every bar. He decided to copy the flautist's example and ordered strawberry cordial, but it tasted foul and at around five o'clock he went back to drinking beer.

'Haven't seen Dédé either, no. Are you supposed to be meeting him?'

From one end of the neighbourhood to the other, he came up against the same wall of silence. Eventually, at around seven o'clock, someone said to him:

'Wasn't he at the races?'

No sign of Lucile either. He ended up questioning the woman who looked least surly.

'Most likely that she's gone to the country.'

At first he was baffled.

'Does she often go to the country?'

They looked at him and laughed.

'She does, like all women! So best to make the most of it and take a break . . .'

Three or four times he almost gave up. He had even wavered at the entrance to the Métro and descended several steps.

And now, just after half past seven, as he walked along staring at every woman he passed, he happened to look down the quiet Rue de Tilsit. Horse-drawn cabs and a chauffeur-driven car lined the kerb. At the very front stood a grey car, the model and registration number instantly familiar.

It was Dédé's car. There was no one in it. A patrol officer was standing on the corner of the street.

'I'm from the Saint-Georges district police station. I'd like you to do me a favour. If the owner of this car comes back and tries to drive off, could you detain him on some pretext?'

'Do you have your ID?'

Even the police officers in this neighbourhood were suspicious! It was the hour when all the restaurants were full. Since Dédé wasn't at Le Coq – he had just checked – he was probably eating somewhere else. Maigret went into a working-class eatery where people pushed past him and he was sent away with a flea in his ear:

'Dédé? . . . Never heard of him . . .'

Neither had anyone heard of him in the brasserie close to the Salle Wagram concert hall.

Twice, Maigret went to check that the car was still there.

He was tempted to puncture one of the tyres with a pen-knife as a precaution but was deterred by the presence of the patrol officer, who had many more years than him under his belt.

And now he was pushing open the door of a little Italian restaurant. He asked the usual question:

'You wouldn't happen to have seen the count?'

'Bob? . . . No . . . Not yesterday, or today . . .'

'What about Dédé?'

The room was small and fairly elegant, with red plush banquettes. At the back, a partition which almost reached the ceiling screened off a sort of private dining room from the main restaurant, and a man in a check suit appeared in the doorway. He had a ruddy face and very blond hair with a centre parting.

'What is it?' he asked, addressing not Maigret but the owner who was behind the bar.

'He's asking for the count or Dédé . . .'

The man in the check suit started moving towards him, his mouth full, his napkin in his hand. He came right up to Maigret, calmly, pausing to look him up and down.

'Well?' he asked.

And while Maigret was trying to think of an answer:

'I'm Dédé.'

Maigret had rehearsed a number of scenarios in case he found himself face to face with the man, but he improvised a new one.

'I arrived yesterday,' he stated awkwardly.

'Arrived from where?'

'From Lyon. I live in Lyon.'

'Now that's interesting!'

'I'm looking for a friend, someone I was at school with . . .'

'If it's a school friend, it's not me you want.'

'It's Count d'Anseval . . . Bob . . .'

'Well, well, well!'

He was not smiling. He ran his tongue over his teeth, thinking.

'And where have you been looking for Bob?'

'Everywhere. He wasn't at his hotel.'

'Because when you two were at school, he gave you the address of his hotel, did he?'

'A friend gave me the address.'

Dédé signalled imperceptibly to the barman.

'Well! Since you're a friend of Bob's, you must have a drink with us. It just so happens that this evening we're having a little family party.'

He beckoned Maigret to follow him into the private dining room. There was food and wine on the table, champagne in a silver bucket, flute glasses. The other guests were a woman in black, her elbows on the table, and a man with a broken nose and a bovine expression, who rose slowly, with the air of a boxer about to enter the ring.

'This is Albert, a friend.'

And he gave Albert a peculiar look, the same look he had given the owner. He did not raise his voice, still did not smile, and yet Maigret had the feeling that he was mocking him somehow.

'Lucile, Bob's girl.'

Maigret noticed the scar on her very beautiful, very

expressive face. As he leaned over to say good evening, the young woman's eyes filled with tears which she wiped away with her handkerchief.

'Take no notice. She's just lost her father. So she's crying into the champagne. Angelino! Another glass and a plate!'

This frosty cordiality was creepy, ominous, sinister even. Maigret turned around and had the distinct feeling that there was no escape without the permission of the little man in the check suit.

'So, you've come from Lyon to meet up with your old friend Bob?'

'That's not the only reason. I had business in Paris. A friend told me that Bob was here. I lost touch with him years ago.'

'Years, eh! Well, to your health! A friend of Bob's is a friend of ours. Drink up, Lucile!'

She obeyed, her hand trembling so badly that the glass knocked against her teeth.

'She received a telegram this afternoon telling her that her father had died. It's always upsetting. Show us the telegram, Lucile.'

She looked at him in surprise.

'Show the gentleman . . .'

She rummaged in her bag.

'I must have left it in my room.'

'Do you like ravioli? The owner is making his special dish. What's your name, by the way?'

'Jules.'

'I like that. Jules. It sounds good. So, Jules my friend, what do you have to say for yourself?'

'I'd like to have seen Bob before leaving.'

'Because you're going back to Bordeaux soon?'

'Lyon.'

'Oh! Yes, Lyon! Lovely city! I'm sure Bob will be very sorry to have missed you. Especially as he's very fond of his old school friends. Put yourself in his shoes. School friends are decent people. I bet you're a decent person. What do you reckon this gentleman does for a living, Lucile?'

'I don't know.'

'Think! Me, I'll bet he's a pig farmer.'

Was it an idle guess? Why that word 'pig', a derogatory word in some circles for the police? Was he sending the others a warning?

'I work in insurance,' muttered Maigret, playing the part to the hilt, for he had no other option.

The next course was served. The waiter brought another bottle, which Dédé must have ordered with a gesture.

'It's strange how people bump into one another. You arrive in Paris out of the blue, you vaguely remember an old school friend and you run into someone who gives you his address. Anyone else might have searched for ten years, especially as there isn't a soul in the neighbourhood who knows the name d'Anseval. Take me, for example. Angelino and the owner have known me for years. Ask them my name and they'll tell you I'm Dédé. Just Dédé. Stop bawling, Lucile! The gentleman will think you don't know how to behave at the table.'

The other man, the one with the boxer's nose, said nothing. He ate and drank with a mulish expression, now and then giving a sort of silent snigger, as if he found the garage owner's jokes very entertaining.

Lucile checked the time on a little gold watch that dangled from her belt on a chain, and Dédé reassured her:

'You'll catch your train, don't worry.'

He explained to Maigret:

'I'm taking her to the local train later to make sure she gets there in time for the funeral. Funny thing, life. Today, her old man snuffs it, and I back the winner at Longchamp. I'm rolling in dough so I'm putting on a little party. But Bob's not here to raise a glass.'

'Has he gone away?'

'Like you say, Jules, he's gone away. But we'll try and arrange for you to see him later anyway.'

Lucile began sobbing again.

'Drink up, sweetheart! Drown your sorrows. Who'd have thought that she was such a sensitive creature? For two hours I've been doing everything I can to cheer her up. Fathers have to die sooner or later, don't they? How long is it since you last saw him, Lucile?'

'Shut up!'

'Same again, Angelino. What about the soufflé? Tell the boss not to ruin the soufflé. To your good health, Jules!'

No matter how much Maigret drank, his glass was always full, and Dédé had an almost menacing way of filling it and clinking glasses.

'What's the name of your friend who gave you Bob's address?'

'Bertrand.'

'He must be pretty well informed. Not only did he give you the low-down on old Bob, but he sent you to the garage.'

So he already knew that someone had been prowling around Rue des Acacias asking questions about him. He must have dropped by in the late afternoon.

'What garage?' mumbled Maigret.

'I thought you said something about a garage. Wasn't it me you were asking for when you came in here?'

'I knew that you and Bob were friends.'

'You Lyon boys are clever! To your good health, Jules! Let's drink Russian style! Drain your glass in one! Come on! Don't you like that?'

The boxer in his corner seemed jubilant, whereas Lucile, forgetting her grief for a moment, seemed to be increasingly anxious. Two or three times, Maigret thought he caught her flashing Dédé a questioning look.

What were they going to do with him? Dédé clearly had something in mind. He was growing more and more jovial, in his own way, without smiling and with a strange glint in his eye. Sometimes he sought approval from the other two, like an actor who feels on top form.

'Whatever happens, I must keep a cool head,' Maigret said to himself as he was forced to drink one glass of champagne after another.

He wasn't armed. He was strong, but he couldn't take on two men like Dédé and the boxer in particular. He was distinctly aware of an icy resolve in the pair of them.

Did they know he was from the police? Probably.

Perhaps Lucile had dropped into Rue Brey and heard about the insistent visitor who had been there earlier? Perhaps they had even been expecting him?

And yet there was a good reason for this celebration. Dédé had declared that he was feeling flush, and it was clearly true; he had that excited air of those of his kind who suddenly find their wallets bulging.

The races? Dédé must be a regular, but Maigret would have sworn that he hadn't been anywhere near Longchamp that day.

As for Lucile's tears, it wasn't because of her father's death that she kept bursting into sobs. Why did she well up every time Bob's name was mentioned?

It was ten o'clock, and they were still at the table, the champagne still flowing. And Maigret continued to fight off the drunkenness.

'Do you mind if I make a telephone call, Jules?'

The telephone booth was to the left, in the main dining room, and, from where he sat, Maigret could see him. Dédé had to request two or three numbers before getting through to the person he was calling. His lips could be seen moving, but it was impossible to guess what he was saying. Lucile looked worried, while the boxer, who had lit a huge cigar, was smiling blissfully and giving Maigret the occasional wink.

Inside the glass booth, Dédé appeared to be giving orders, emphasizing certain words. There was no trace of merriment on his face now.

'Apologies, but I didn't want you to miss seeing your friend Bob.'

Lucile, at the end of her tether, burst into tears, burying her face in her handkerchief.

'Was it Bob you were telephoning?'

'Not exactly, but as good as. I've arranged for the two of you to meet up. That's the main thing, isn't it? You're very keen to see him, aren't you?'

His words must have been very witty, for the boxer looked ecstatic and even let out a sort of chuckle of admiration.

Did they imagine that Maigret didn't understand what they meant? The count was dead, or almost. So when Dédé promised Maigret he would get the two of them together . . .

'I also need to make a telephone call,' he said, sounding as casual as possible.

Despite Maxime Le Bret's advice, he had just decided to inform his station: he didn't dare talk to the police from a different neighbourhood. It would be Besson on duty, or Colombani, playing cards with Sergeant Duffieu. He simply needed to drag things out to give his colleagues the time to get there and position themselves near the car.

They wouldn't dare do anything to him inside the restaurant. There were still customers whose voices could be heard on the other side of the partition, and while a lot of them were from the underworld, there must be some who weren't.

'Who do you need to telephone?'

'My wife.'

'So your wife's here with you? Married, eh? Do you hear that, Lucile? Jules is spoken for. He's not for you! No point playing footsie under the table. To your health, Jules! No need to get up. Angelino will make the call for you. Angelino! Which hotel is your missus staying at?'

The waiter stood waiting for Maigret's reply, and he too seemed to be relishing the situation.

'It's not urgent.'

'Are you sure? Won't she be worried? She might think that something's happened to you and have the police out looking for you. A bottle, Angelino! Or rather no, let's have cognac, now. It's time. In balloon snifters. I'm sure our friend Jules loves cognac.'

For a second, Maigret thought of jumping up and making a beeline for the door, but he realized that they'd block his path. More than likely the two men were armed. They probably had friends, if not accomplices, in the restaurant, and Angelino, the waiter, would have no hesitation in tripping him up.

Then Maigret felt a calmness, a clear-headed calmness, extremely clear-headed, despite all the champagne and the cognac he had been forced to drink. From time to time he too checked his watch. It was not so long since he had been policing the railway stations and he knew the timetables of the main trains by heart.

Dédé had not been speaking idly when he had talked of a train. They really were leaving, possibly all three of them. They must already have their tickets. And each half-hour that passed reduced the possibilities. The Le Havre train, which might have been taking them to some ocean liner, had left Saint-Lazare ten minutes ago. At Gare de l'Est, the Strasbourg train would be leaving in around twenty minutes.

Dédé was not a man to go and lie low in some rural hidey-hole where he would eventually be tracked down. He had his car outside, parked by the kerb in Rue de Tilsit.

They were leaving with no luggage. They probably planned to abandon the car too.

'Don't drink any more, Lucile. If I know you, you'll end up throwing up all over the tablecloth, and that's not nice. Angelino, the bill!'

And, pretending to believe that Maigret had made as if to take his wallet from his pocket:

'No way! I told you that this was a little family party . . .'

He proudly opened a wallet stuffed with thousand-franc notes. He didn't even look at the bill, and pressed one of the notes into Angelino's hand saying:

'Keep the change!'

He must have been very sure of himself.

'And now, folks, let's go. We'll drive Lucile to the station, then we'll go and find Bob. Are you happy, Jules? Can you stand up? Our friend Albert will help you. Yes, he will! Take his arm, Albert, while I look after the young lady.'

It was half past eleven. That end of Avenue de Wagram was poorly lit; the bright lights were further down, towards Place des Ternes. The owner watched them leave with a strange expression, and before they had taken ten steps, he hastily pulled the shutters down, even though there were still two or three customers inside.

'Hold on to him, Albert. We don't want him falling on his face, otherwise his friend Bob won't recognize him. This way, ladies and gentlemen!'

If there had been a police officer on the corner, Maigret

would have called for help, because he knew only too well what lay in store. He had heard too much, seen too much. He realized that his fate had been sealed from the moment he'd set foot inside the Italian restaurant.

There was no patrol officer in sight. He noticed two or three girls silhouetted in the dark on the other side of the road. At the end of the avenue, an empty tram stood at the terminus, its windows casting a syrupy, yellowish light.

Maigret dared to hope that his companions would not shoot. They needed time to jump into the car and get out of the neighbourhood before the alarm was raised.

Knife? Probably. It was the fashion. And Albert the boxer had pinned his right arm to his side under the pretence of helping him to keep upright.

A pity that Maigret hadn't been able to puncture one of the tyres earlier. Had he waited a few minutes until the police officer had his back turned, the situation would have been different.

It was almost midnight. There were two more trains that night, one for Belgium, from Gare du Nord, and the Ventimiglia train from Gare de Lyon. But Ventimiglia was a long way away.

Madame Maigret must be waiting up for him, sewing; Justin Minard would be playing the double bass at the Brasserie Clichy, where the number of the piece was written on a card. Had he managed to shake off Germaine? Maigret would have sworn that she was there, in the brasserie, and that the musician would be wondering what to do with her.

There wasn't a soul, not a cab to be seen in Rue de Tilsit. Only the grey car parked by the kerb. After settling Lucile in the rear seat, Dédé slid behind the wheel and started up the engine.

Perhaps they wanted to drive him to an even more deserted spot, by the Seine or the Saint-Martin canal, so they could throw his body into the water?

Maigret had no wish to die, and yet he was somehow resigned. He would do his utmost to defend himself, but that was not much. His left hand in his pocket clutched a bunch of keys.

If only the engine had refused to start! But after a few splutters, it was ticking over and the car was quivering on its wheels.

The goatskin jacket was on the seat, but Dédé didn't bother to put it on. Was he going to beat Maigret up, or would it be the boxer who was standing behind Maigret and still gripping his right arm?

The moment had come, and it is just possible that Maigret inwardly prayed: 'Please God let me . . .'

As if by chance, they suddenly heard voices. Two fairly drunk men in evening dress were weaving down Avenue de Wagram, the knobs of their canes protruding from the pockets of their black cloaks. They were humming the chorus that was all the rage in the cabarets.

'Come on, Jules!' said Dédé with a haste that Maigret just managed to detect.

Then, as Maigret lifted his right foot to clamber into the car, he received a violent blow to the head. He was quick-witted enough to duck, and that cushioned the shock. He

117

thought he heard footsteps approaching, voices, an engine backfiring, before he lost consciousness.

When he opened his eyes, first of all he saw legs, patent-leather shoes, then pallid faces in the dark. There seemed to be a lot of them, a whole crowd, and yet, a little later, he was surprised to see that there were only five people surrounding him.

One of the faces was that of a plump, flabby, placid girl who had probably been soliciting on the other side of the avenue and been drawn over by the commotion. He had seen her two or three times that afternoon, at her station, and she probably hadn't had much luck if she was still looking for custom at that hour. The two revellers were also there, and one of them, leaning over him, was stubbornly questioning him, most likely still drunk:

'Feeling better, my friend? Tell me, are you feeling better now?'

Why was there a basket and why was there a smell of violets? He tried to raise himself up on one elbow. The reveller helped him. Then he spotted an elderly flower-seller who was complaining:

'Those thugs again! If this carries on . . .'

And a hotel bellboy in a red uniform rushed over, saying:

'I'll go and fetch the police!'

'I'm fine, thank you!'

Maigret asked as if in a trance:

'What time is it?'

'Five past midnight.'

'I have to make a telephone call.'

'Of course, my friend! In a minute. Someone's bringing you a telephone. They're just getting it.'

He had lost his hat and his hair was plastered to the top of his head. That thug Albert must have delivered his punch with a knuckleduster. If it hadn't been for the two night owls, he would most likely have finished him off, and if Maigret hadn't ducked . . .

Again, he said:

'I have to make a telephone call.'

He managed to raise himself on to all fours, and blood dripped from his head on to the pavement, while one of the revellers exclaimed:

'He's drunk. It's priceless! He's still drunk!'

'I assure you I have to—'

'. . . make a telephone call . . . Yes, my friend . . . Do you hear, Armand? . . . Go and get him a telephone.'

And the girl, becoming indignant:

'Can't you see he's delirious. You'd do better to call a doctor.'

'Do you know of one around here?'

'There's one in Rue de l'Étoile.'

But the bellboy was already back, all excited, showing two police officers on bicycles the way. The others stood aside. The officers leaned over.

'I have to make a telephone call . . .' repeated Maigret.

It was funny. He hadn't felt drunk all evening, but now his words were slurred and his thoughts muddled. Only one remained clear, imperative.

He stuttered, annoyed at being there, on the ground, in that ludicrous position, unable to stand up:

'Police . . . Look in my wallet . . . Saint-Georges district
. . . Telephone Gare du Nord immediately . . . The Brussels
train . . . in a few minutes . . . They have a car . . .'

One of the officers had gone over to stand beneath the
gas lamp to examine the contents of Maigret's wallet.

'It's true, Germain.'

'Listen . . . Hurry . . . They've got their tickets . . . A
woman in black, with a scar on her cheek . . . One of the
men is wearing a check suit . . . The other one has a broken
nose.'

'Will you go, Germain?'

The police station was in Rue de l'Étoile, not far away.
One of the officers jumped on to his bicycle. The bellboy,
who hadn't heard much of what they'd said, asked:

'Is he a cop?'

Maigret lost consciousness again, while one of the
revellers struggled to form the words:

'I tell you he's drunk as a skunk!'

# 7. Madame Maigret's Laughter

He was still trying to push them away, but his hand was limp, with no strength. He wished they would just leave him alone. Had he asked them to? He couldn't remember. There were so many things in his head that it hurt a little.

Above all he was certain of one thing: he absolutely must be allowed to see this thing through to the end. The end of what? Good Lord! How difficult people found it to understand him! *To the end!*

But they were treating him like a child, or an invalid. No one asked his opinion. The most annoying thing was that they were talking about his case in front of him, as if he were incapable of understanding. Because he was still lying on the ground like a giant crushed insect? There had been legs around him, then the ambulance. He had been perfectly aware that it was an ambulance and he had struggled. Can't a person receive a blow to the head without being carted off to hospital?

He had also recognized the dark gates of Beaujon Hospital, the arch with a very powerful electric light that hurt his eyes; people were calmly coming and going, a tall young man in a white coat seemed to be laughing at everyone.

Maigret knew that he was the junior doctor, didn't he? A nurse was cutting the hair on the top of his head, and the doctor was whispering sweet nothings. She was very pretty in her uniform. From the way they were looking at each other, they must have been making love just before Maigret's arrival.

He didn't want to vomit, but he did, because of the ether.

'That'll teach him,' he said to himself.

What were they giving him to drink? He refused to drink. He needed to think. Hadn't the officer on a bicycle told them that he was a policeman in charge of an important case, a *confidential* case?

No one believed him. It was the chief inspector's fault. He didn't want to be carried. And why did Madame Maigret burst out laughing as she yanked back the sheets?

He was sure she had laughed, with a nervous laugh that he'd never heard before, then for a long time he heard her coming in and out of the bedroom making as little noise as possible.

Could he have acted differently? If only they would let him think. If only they'd give him a pencil and paper. Any old scrap of paper, yes. Good.

Now, if this line is Rue Chaptal . . . It's very short . . . Good . . . It's just after one o'clock in the morning, and there's no one in the street . . .

Wrong, there is someone. There's Dédé, at the wheel of his car. And Dédé has kept the engine running. There could be two reasons for that. The first, that he has only stopped for a few minutes. The second, that he's expecting to have to make a quick getaway. And it's difficult to start cars up again, especially when it's chilly – and April nights are chilly.

No one must interrupt him! A line, then. A little square for the Balthazars' house. He called it the Balthazars' residence, because it rang truer than the Gendreaus'. Ultimately, it's all the Balthazar family, Balthazar money, the Balthazar saga.

If Dédé's car is there, there's a reason. And that reason is that it has probably dropped the count off and is waiting to pick him up when he leaves.

This is very serious. Don't interrupt . . . There's no need to put things on his head or boil water in the kitchen. He can hear water being boiled. People are always boiling water and it's very annoying, it stops you thinking.

On other occasions when the count had visited Lise, had Dédé driven him there? It's crucial to find out. Otherwise, that nocturnal visit was a one-off call with a specific purpose.

Why had Madame Maigret burst out laughing? What was so funny about him? Did she also think that he'd been larking around with girls?

Justin Minard was the one who'd slept with Germaine. She certainly didn't intend to let go of him and would probably make his life a misery for a long time. What about Carmen? He'd never met her. There were lots of people he'd never met.

It wasn't fair. When you're conducting a *confidential* investigation, you should be allowed to see everyone, to see them from inside.

They must give him back his pencil. This square was a bedroom. Lise's bedroom, of course. The furniture wasn't important. There's no point drawing furniture. It would only confuse things. Only the bedside table, because there was a pistol either on top of it or in the drawer.

Now, the crucial question: was Lise in bed or wasn't she? Was she expecting the count or not? If she was in bed, she must have taken the pistol out of the drawer.

If only they'd stop squeezing his head, damn it! You can't think when someone's pressing down on your head with some heavy object.

How come it was broad daylight? Who's this? There's a man in the room, a short, bald man, someone he knows but whose name eludes him. Madame Maigret whispers. A cold object is slipped into his mouth.

For pity's sake, gentlemen! . . . In a while he's going to have to go into the witness box and, if he babbles incoherently, Lise Gendreau will burst out laughing saying that he can't possibly understand because he's not a member of the Hoche club.

He must concentrate on the square. The little circle is Lise. Remember it's only the women in the family who have inherited the character of old Balthazar, the recluse who lived in Avenue du Bois. He's the one who said it, and he should know.

So why does she rush over to the window, draw back the curtains and cry for help?

Hold on, inspector . . . Don't forget Minard, the flautist, because he has just changed everything . . .

There wasn't time for anyone to leave the house when Minard rang the doorbell, and while he was arguing with Louis, a man's voice on the stairs shouted:

'*Hurry up, Louis!*'

And Dédé's car drove off. But hold on! It didn't disappear altogether. It drove around the block. So Dédé was definitely waiting for someone.

When he came back, was he content to just cruise down the street to have a look? Or did he stop? Did the person he was waiting for get into the car?

Hell and damnation, why couldn't they leave him alone! He doesn't want to drink any more. He's had enough. He's working. Do you hear! I'm *work-ing!*

*I'm re-con-struct-ing!*

He feels hot. He struggles. He will not allow anyone to laugh at him, no one, not even his wife. It's enough to make you cry. He really feels like crying. It's pointless humiliating him like this. Just because he's sitting on the pavement, that's no reason to treat him with disdain and laugh at everything he says.

He won't be put in charge of any more cases. Already they were uncertain about this one. Is it his fault if you sometimes have to drink with people to find out what makes them tick?

'Jules . . .'

He shakes his head.

'Jules! Wake up . . .'

He'll punish them by refusing to open his eyes. He clenches his jaw. He must look fierce.

'Jules, it's . . .'

And another voice says:

'Well, Maigret, my boy?'

He has forgotten his vow. He sits up abruptly and feels as if he has banged his head on the ceiling. He automatically raises his hand to his head and finds that it is encased in a thick bandage.

'I'm sorry, sir . . .'

'I'm sorry I woke you.'

'I wasn't asleep.'

His wife is there, smiling at him, and is making unintelligible signs behind Monsieur Le Bret's back.

'What time is it?'

'Half past ten. I heard what had happened when I arrived at the office.'

'Have they written a report?'

A report on him! How humiliating. Usually he's the one who writes reports, and he knows the formula:

*Last night, at 11.45 pm, while on patrol in Avenue de Wagram, we were hailed by . . .*

Something along the lines of:

*. . . an individual lying on the ground stating that his name was Maigret, Jules, Amédée, François . . .*

As for the chief inspector, he was looking dapper in pearl grey from head to toe, a flower in his buttonhole. His breath smelled of his early-morning tipple of port.

'The Gare du Nord police arrested them in the nick of time.'

Goodness! He had almost forgotten that lot! He was tempted to say, like the flautist: 'It doesn't matter.'

And it was true. It wasn't Dédé who mattered, or Lucile, or even less the boxer who'd hit him over the head, with 'a blunt instrument' as the report probably said.

It was the embarrassment of being in bed in front of his boss. He poked a leg out.

'Don't get out of bed.'

'I'm fine, I assure you.'

'That's what the doctor said too. All the same, you need a few days' rest.'

'Never!'

He knew they wanted to take his case away from him. But he wasn't going to let them trample all over him.

'Calm down, Maigret.'

'I am calm, perfectly calm. And I know what I'm saying. There's no reason why I can't walk or go outside.'

'There's no rush. I understand your hurry, but as far as your case is concerned, we'll do whatever you feel is necessary.'

He had said 'your case', because he was a man of the world. Without thinking he lit a cigarette then glanced at Madame Maigret in embarrassment.

'Don't worry. My husband smokes a pipe all day long and even in bed.'

'That's a good idea, give me a pipe.'

'Are you sure?'

'Did the doctor say I mustn't smoke?'

'He didn't mention it.'

'So?'

She had put everything she'd found in his pockets on top of the dressing table, and she began to fill a pipe for him. She held it out to him along with a match.

'I'll leave you to it,' she said, making her exit and retreating to the kitchen.

Maigret tried to recall everything he had thought of during the night. He only had a vague recollection and yet he had the feeling he'd been close to the truth. Maxime Le Bret sat down on a chair; he was clearly worried. He became even more so when his secretary announced slowly, between two puffs:

'Count d'Anseval is dead.'

'Are you certain?'

'I don't have any evidence, but I'd swear to it.'

'Dead . . . how?'

'He's the one who got shot.'

'Rue Chaptal?'

Maigret nodded.

'Do you think that it's Richard Gendreau who . . .'

The question is too specific. Maigret hasn't reached that point yet. He remembers his square, with the little crosses.

'There was a pistol on the bedside table, or in the drawer. Lise Gendreau cried for help from the window. Then she was dragged backwards. And then a shot was heard.'

'What's Dédé doing mixed up in all this?'

'He was in the street, at the wheel of the De Dion-Bouton.'

'Has he admitted it?'

'There's no need for him to admit it.'

'What about the woman?'

'She's the mistress of the count, who's generally known as Bob. Anyway, you know that as well as I do.'

Maigret would have liked to be rid of the ridiculous turban that was making his head feel heavy.

'What's been done with them?' he asked.

'They've been taken to headquarters for the time being.'

'Until when?'

'For the moment they've simply been charged with carrying out an armed attack on a public thoroughfare. They could probably be charged with robbery too.'

'Why?'

'This Dédé had forty-nine one-thousand franc notes in his pockets.'

'He didn't steal them.'

The inspector must have read his thoughts, for he became increasingly glum.

'Do you mean they were given to him?'

'Yes.'

'To keep him quiet?'

'Yes. Dédé disappeared for the whole of yesterday afternoon. When he resurfaced, so to speak, he was jubilant, impatient to spend some of the money swelling his pockets. While Lucile was crying over the death of her lover, he was celebrating his new-found fortune. I was with them.'

Poor Le Bret! He could not get used to Maigret's transformation. He was like those parents who treat their child like a baby and then suddenly see before them a man reasoning like an adult.

Who knew? Watching him, Maigret had a vague suspicion. Gradually, this suspicion turned into a conviction.

If Le Bret had entrusted him with the case, it was in the certainty – the hope – that he would find nothing.

This is what had happened. Monsieur Le Bret-Courcelles, the socialite, had absolutely no desire to see one of his circle, a friend from his club, being inconvenienced, even less a close friend of his wife's, a Balthazar Coffee heiress.

That damned flautist who'd come poking his nose into something that was none of his business!

Were the goings-on in an upstairs bedroom in a private house in Rue Chaptal of any interest to the papers, the public, or even juries made up chiefly of small shop-keepers and bank clerks?

But on the other hand, Chief Inspector Le Bret couldn't very well tear up a statement in front of his secretary.

'. . . you understand, Maigret, my boy . . .'

Discretion. No scandal. Extreme caution. The best way to ensure that Maigret found out nothing. Then, after a few days, he would have been greeted with smiling condescension.

'. . . Come, come, it's not important. You mustn't lose heart. You did all you could. It's not your fault if that flautist is a madman who dreamed the whole thing up. Back to work, my boy! I promise you that the next big case will be yours.'

Right now, he was worried, naturally. He might even be wishing that Maigret hadn't softened the blow by ducking in time? If he hadn't, he would have been out of action for days, if not weeks.

How the devil had the fellow found out so much?

He cleared his throat and murmured in as detached a tone as possible:

'In other words, you're accusing Richard Gendreau of murder.'

'Not necessarily him. It could have been his sister who fired. It is also possible that it was Louis. Don't forget that the flautist must have rung the bell, then stood knocking on the door for ages before Louis opened it, and when he did, he was fully dressed.'

It was a ray of hope. What a relief if it was the butler who had done it!

'Don't you think that the last hypothesis sounds the most plausible?'

He blushed because Maigret couldn't help staring at him insistently. He began to speak volubly.

'As far as I'm concerned, that's how I'd gladly see things . . .'

He said *gladly*, and the word was delicious; Maigret acknowledged it in passing.

'I don't know precisely what business brought the count to the house . . .'

'It wasn't the first time.'

'As you have already said, and I was surprised. He was a desperado. His father still retained a certain dignity, even though he'd lost all his money. He lived in a little apartment in the Latin Quarter and carefully avoided the people he had known in his youth.'

'Did he work?'

'No. Not exactly.'

'What did he live on?'

'He sold items that he'd salvaged from the disaster as and when he needed to: paintings, a snuffbox, a family jewel. Perhaps some people who had known his father and used to hunt at the chateau discreetly sent him a little money? Bob, on the other hand, became a sort of anarchist. He flaunted himself in the seediest places. At one point, he got a job as a bellboy at the Voisin restaurant, just to embarrass his family's friends by accepting tips from them. He went off the rails in the end, mixing with the likes of Lucile and Dédé. Now where was I?'

Maigret said nothing.

'Oh, yes! He was bound to have gone to the Gendreaus' that night with dishonourable intentions.'

'Why?'

'The fact that he was driven there by Dédé, who waited for him in the street without even turning off his engine, suggests that was the case.'

'But he was expected.'

'How do you know?'

'Do you think he'd have been allowed up to a young lady's bedroom otherwise? And why was Louis fully dressed at one o'clock in the morning?'

'Let's suppose he was expected, which doesn't mean he was welcome. Perhaps he had indeed announced his visit.'

'To the bedroom, remember.'

'Very well! I'll admit too that Lise behaved recklessly with him. We should not judge her.'

Well! Well!

'It is possible that the two of them had an affair. After all, he is still heir to the Anseval name, and his grandparents were the masters of the chateau bought by old Balthazar, who was merely one of their peasant farmers.'

'That might impress the pedlar's granddaughter.'

'Why not? Mind you, it's also plausible that, on discovering the kind of life he was leading, she wanted to save him.'

Why was Maigret becoming furious? He had the feeling that his entire investigation was being reflected back to him in a distortion mirror. Nor did he like the insinuating tone of the chief inspector, who sounded as if he was giving a lecture.

'There's another possibility,' he said quietly.

'What's that?'

'That Mademoiselle Gendreau-Balthazar wanted to add a title to her fortune. It's all very well having acquired the Château d'Anseval. But perhaps she felt a little like an interloper? I too spent my childhood in the shadow of a chateau, where my father was the estate manager. I remember how desperate some of the nouveaux riches were to be invited for the hunt.'

'Are you insinuating that she wanted to marry—'

'Bob d'Anseval, why not?'

'I do not wish to discuss this question, but that sounds to me like a very audacious supposition.'

'That's not what the maid thinks.'

'You questioned the maid, even though . . .'

He nearly added 'even though I advised against it'.

Which was tantamount to saying: 'against my orders!'

But he didn't, and Maigret went on:

'I even sort of kidnapped her. She's just around the corner from here.'

'Did she disclose anything to you?'

'She doesn't know anything for certain, other than that Mademoiselle Gendreau had got it into her head to become a countess.'

Le Bret gave a resigned shrug. It clearly weighed heavily on his heart to see people of his world throwing their dignity to the winds.

'Supposing you're right. That still doesn't alter the facts. Will you admit that Bob might have behaved like a swine?'

'We know nothing of what happened in that bedroom, except that a shot was fired.'

'You have reached the same conclusions as I have. A man behaves in the way that we know he was capable of behaving. The young lady's brother is in the house, and so is the butler. She shouts for help. One of them hears, rushes upstairs and, in his indignation, grabs the pistol which you yourself say is on the bedside table.'

Maigret now appeared to be in agreement. But he retorted softly, puffing on his pipe, one of the most enjoyable he had ever smoked:

'What would you have done in that man's shoes? Supposing that you were still holding the gun, the "smoking gun" as it's called in the papers. On the floor there's a dead or seriously wounded man.'

'Assuming he was wounded, I'd have called a doctor.'

'They didn't.'

'So you infer that he was dead?'

Maigret patiently pursued his train of thought, and he too seemed to be groping in the dark.

'Just then, there's a knock on the door. It's a passer-by who heard a cry for help.'

'Admit, dear Maigret, that it is disagreeable to have some passer-by meddling in your business.'

'Someone shouted from the staircase:

'"*Hurry up, Louis!*"

'What does that mean?'

He was barely aware that he was steering the conversation now; their roles were in a way reversed and his superior was increasingly uncomfortable.

'The man could not be completely dead. Or again, Lise was having hysterics. I don't know. I suppose that in a crisis, people tend to panic somewhat.'

'Louis punched the intruder in the face and shoved him out into the street.'

'He shouldn't have.'

'And nobody should have panicked. Naturally, they realized that the fellow they'd just thrashed would go to the police. And the police would be bound to come round asking for an explanation.'

'Which you did.'

'They only had a few minutes before them. They could have telephoned the authorities and said:

'"This is what happened. It's not a murder but an accident. We had no option but to shoot a maniac who was threatening us."

'I think that's how you would have acted, inspector, wouldn't you?'

How it changed the situation being here, in his room, in his bed, instead of at the office. Behind the baize door of the police station, he would not have dared say a quarter of the things he had just said. He had a thumping headache, but that was secondary. Madame Maigret, in the kitchen, must have been terrified hearing him talk with such assurance. He even became aggressive.

'Well, sir! That is what *they* didn't do. But this is what they did do. First of all, they moved the body, or the wounded man, to goodness knows where. They probably took him to one of the rooms above the stables, since they are the only ones I wasn't shown.'

'That's only a supposition.'

'Based on the fact that the body was no longer there when I arrived.'

'And what if Bob had left under his own steam?'

'His friend Dédé would not have had fifty thousand francs in his pocket yesterday, and what's more he certainly wouldn't have decided to leave for Belgium with Lucile.'

'Perhaps you're right.'

'So, our people in Rue Chaptal had around half an hour. That gave them enough time to clean up the place and remove every trace of what had happened. And they had an idea that was almost a stroke of genius. Wasn't the best way to dismiss the flautist's testimony to claim it was the ramblings of a drunkard, and to show that the room he was pointing to was unoccupied? That had another advantage. Perhaps, despite everything, Lise Gendreau was a bundle of nerves, as they say. Show her in bed and claim that she was asleep? Better to show her on her feet and assert that she hadn't heard anything? That was just as risky.

'They bundled her into a maid's room that was miraculously empty. Would a nobody from the local police station know the difference?

'They simply needed to claim that she was away at her chateau in the Nièvre. Didn't hear a thing! Didn't see a thing! A shot? Where?

'People who roam the streets at one o'clock in the morning are often not in their right minds.

'Next morning, in broad daylight, who would dare accuse the Gendreau-Balthazars?'

'You are harsh, Maigret.'

He sighed and stood up.

'But perhaps you're right. I'm going to confer with the head of the Sûreté.'

'Do you think that's necessary?'

'If a murder really has taken place, and you have finally convinced me—'

'Sir!' said Maigret in a softer, almost imploring voice.

'Yes?'

'Could you possibly wait twenty-four hours?'

'Earlier, you almost accused me of not acting fast enough.'

'I assure you that I can get up. Look.'

And despite Le Bret's gesture of protest, he emerged from the sheets, a little dazed, and managed to stand up, rather embarrassed all the same to be in his nightshirt in front of his boss.

'This is my first case.'

'And I congratulate you on your zeal—'

'If you inform the Sûreté right away, the chief's squad will take over the case.'

'Probably. First of all, if Bob has been killed, we have to find the body.'

'If it's a question of a dead body, it can wait, can't it?'

The roles were reversed once again, and the inspector turned his head away to hide a smile.

Maigret, so passionate earlier, in his nightshirt with its collar embroidered in red, suddenly looked like an overgrown child deprived of a treat he had been promised.

'I don't need this thing on my head.'

He tried to rip off his dressing.

'I can wind up this case on my own. Just give me permission to go and question Dédé and Lucile, especially Lucile. What did they say?'

'This morning, when the duty officer questioned him, he asked: "Is Jules dead?" I presume he was talking about you.'

'If I haven't succeeded by this time tomorrow, you can hand the case over to the Sûreté.'

Alarmed, Madame Maigret had opened the door a fraction and remained there standing guard, staring at her husband on his feet.

There was a ring at the door. She crossed the room to go and open it, and whispering could be heard coming from the landing.

When she came back, alone, Maigret asked:

'Who is it?'

She gestured to him, but he didn't understand and, since he insisted, she finally admitted:

'The musician.'

'I'm off,' said Le Bret. 'I can't in all decency refuse your request.'

'Excuse me, sir, I'd also like . . . Given the way the situation has developed, and given that the Sûreté would do so, may I speak to Mademoiselle Gendreau if necessary?'

'I imagine that you'll be tactful? But do be careful.'

Maigret was delighted. He heard the door close, then, while he was hunting around for his trousers, Justin Minard came into the room, followed by Madame Maigret. The musician looked woeful, worried.

'Are you hurt?'

'Not really.'

'I have some bad news for you.'

'Go on.'

'She's gone.'

The flautist's crestfallen expression was so funny that Maigret nearly burst out laughing.

'When?'

'Yesterday evening, or rather last night. She insisted on coming with me to the Brasserie Clichy, claiming that she was crazy about music and that she wanted to hear me play.'

Madame Maigret's presence made it even more difficult for him to own up. She understood and disappeared back into her kitchen.

'She was sitting in the seat that you occupied when you came to see me. I was uncomfortable. Since I hadn't been home for dinner and hadn't set foot in my place all day, I was expecting to see my wife appear at any moment.'

'Did she come?'

'Yes.'

'Did they have an argument?'

'I was sitting at the table having a break between numbers. My wife started it by yanking off Germaine's hat, then she grabbed her chignon.'

'Were they thrown out?'

'Both of them. I was back on stage. The band was playing to keep up appearances, like when a ship's going down, you know? We could hear them fighting outside. When we finished the piece, the owner came to fetch me and asked me to go and sort out my harem, as he called it.'

'Were they waiting for you in the street?'

'Only one. My wife. She dragged me home. She locked up my shoes so I couldn't go out. I came out anyway, an hour ago, and I borrowed the concierge's shoes. Germaine has left the hotel. She came to pick up her suitcase.'

He finished:

'Now what do we do?'

## 8. One Says Nothing, the Other Says Too Much

'Please put on your heavy overcoat, at least,' Madame Maigret had insisted.

In those days, he had two overcoats, a heavy black one with a velvet collar, which he had been trailing around for three years, and a short beige one which he had been hankering after since his youth and had recently splashed out on.

As the two of them left the apartment, he suspected his wife of having whispered in Minard's ear: 'Don't let him out of your sight, whatever you do!'

Although she made fun of him a little, she was fond of the flautist, who was so gentle, polite and self-effacing. The sky was overcast and the beautiful pale grey fluffy clouds promised rain for the first time in ten days or so – showers, or sheets, long hatchings of warm rain that would make Maigret all damp beneath his overcoat and leave him smelling like a wet animal.

He carried his bowler hat in his hand, since it wouldn't fit over the bulky dressing on his head. Minard went with him to the doctor's on Boulevard Voltaire to have the bandages changed for a more discreet dressing.

'Do you absolutely have to go into town?'

The doctor gave him a packet containing pills rolled in yellow powder.

'In case you feel dizzy.'

'How many can I take?'

'Four or five between now and this evening. No more. I'd rather you stayed in bed.'

Maigret wasn't quite sure what to do with the musician, but he didn't want to upset him by sending him home now he no longer needed him. So he sent him to Rue Chaptal, letting him think that he was on a very important mission.

'More or less opposite the Gendreaus' house there's a little restaurant called the Vieux Calvados. I want you to sit at a table and watch what's happening in the house.'

'But suppose you start feeling unwell?'

'I won't be alone.'

Minard stayed with him until they arrived at the gate of police headquarters, Quai de l'Horloge. At that point, Maigret was still full of self-confidence. He even sniffed the odour of the dark arch with delight. Everything was dirty, seedy. This was where each night the officers brought in all the suspicious individuals they had picked up on the streets and where the meat wagons discharged the low-life rounded up during raids.

He entered the guardroom that smelled of barracks and asked if the chief inspector would see him. People seemed to be staring at him oddly, but he didn't dwell on that impression. He said to himself that of course the men here looked down on a humble secretary from a district police station.

'Have a seat.'

There were three officers; one of them was writing, while the others were doing nothing. The chief inspector's office was next door, but no one went to inform him, and no one took any notice of Maigret; they treated him as if he were an outsider. It was so embarrassing that he didn't dare fill his pipe.

After a quarter of an hour, he ventured to ask:

'Is the chief inspector not here?'

'Busy.'

'Where are the people who were picked up last night?'

He hadn't seen anyone in the vast room where they normally herded their victims.

'Upstairs.'

He didn't dare ask permission to go up to Criminal Records. The men were made to go up in a crocodile, like school children, then forced to strip and stand in a line. They were examined one by one and any tattoos and distinguishing marks were noted. Then they were allowed to put their clothes back on before being measured and photographed and lastly having their fingerprints taken.

Was Dédé in the queue among the vagrants and tramps, as cocksure as ever?

In years to come, when he was part of the chief's squad, Maigret would be able to come and go as he pleased anywhere in the building.

Meanwhile, a doctor was examining the women in another room and the sick were sent to the Saint-Lazare infirmary.

'Are you certain that the chief inspector is still busy?'

He had been waiting for more than half an hour. He

thought he caught the three men exchanging amused glances.

'You'll have to wait until he rings.'

'But he doesn't know I'm here. I'm working on an important case. He must be informed.'

'You're from Saint-Georges, aren't you?'

And one of the officers, the one who was writing, glanced at a piece of paper on his desk.

'Jules Maigret?'

'Yes.'

'You'll have to wait, I'm afraid. There's nothing I can do about it.'

There wasn't the slightest sound from the adjacent room where the chief inspector was supposed to be. After Maigret had been waiting for over an hour, he came in, not from his office but from outside.

'Are you Le Bret's secretary?'

At last he was being taken care of instead of being left to twiddle his thumbs like a supplicant.

'You look as if you've been in the wars.'

'It's nothing. I'd like—'

'I know. You want to question a man named Dédé. I think he's come back down. Would you check, Gérard? If he's here, have him brought into my office.'

And to Maigret:

'Come in, please. You may use my office for a while.'

'I also need to question the woman.'

'Fine. Just have the sergeant bring her in.'

Somehow this didn't feel quite right. Maigret had imagined that things would happen differently, but he wasn't worried yet. He wasn't acquainted with the habits of the place and he felt intimidated.

An officer brought Dédé in, then left, and so did the chief inspector, shutting the door behind him.

'Well, Jules?'

The garage owner from Rue des Acacias was wearing the same suit as the night before. Only his tie and bootlaces had been removed, in accordance with the rules, which made him look a little dishevelled. Maigret gingerly sat down at the chief inspector's desk.

'I'm glad we didn't do too much damage,' declared Dédé. 'These gentlemen will tell you: the first thing I said when they brought me here was to ask after you.'

'You knew who I was, didn't you?'

'Of course!'

'And I knew you knew,' said Maigret simply.

'So you suspected that we were going to beat you up? And supposing we'd finished you off completely?'

'Sit down.'

'All right. You can call me Dédé.'

Maigret wasn't used to the lack of formality, but he knew that that was how his colleagues spoke to people here.

'I know a lot of other things too, and I'm sure we'll be able to come to an understanding.'

'I very much doubt it.'

'The count is dead.'

'Do you think so?'

'On the night of the 15th of April, you drove the count, in your car, to Rue Chaptal and you waited for him without switching off the engine.'

'I don't remember.'

'A window opened, a woman screamed and there was a shot. Then you drove off towards Rue Fontaine. You drove round the block. You stopped for quite a while in Rue Victor-Massé, then you cruised down Rue Chaptal one more time, to see if Bob had come out.'

Dédé watched him, smiling calmly.

'Go on,' he said. 'You wouldn't have a cigarette, would you? Those swine took everything I had in my pockets.'

'I only smoke a pipe. You knew why the count had gone to the house.'

'Tell me anyway.'

'You knew that something ugly had happened. The next day, you didn't see anything in the papers. The count didn't return. The day after that, still no news.'

'Now this is getting interesting.'

'You drove over and hung around the street again. Then, guessing what must have occurred, you went to see Richard Gendreau. Not at his house but at his office.'

'And what did I say to that gentleman?'

'That you would keep quiet in exchange for a sum of money, fifty thousand francs probably. Because, knowing why Bob went to Rue Chaptal, you knew why he was killed.'

'Is that all?'

'That's all.'

'What are you offering me?'

'Nothing. I'm asking you to talk.'

'What do you expect me to say?'

'The count knew the Gendreau family. He had visited the young lady several times. Was he her lover?'

'Did you ever see him?'

'No.'

'If you'd seen him, you wouldn't be asking me that question. He wasn't the sort of fellow to let slip an opportunity.'

'There was talk of marriage, wasn't there?'

'You know? I like you. I was actually saying to Lucile: pity he's a fool! How stupid to become a cop when you're built like that and you're not afraid of hard work!'

'Do you prefer prison?'

'To what?'

'If you talk, it's likely that we'll drop the charge of blackmailing Richard Gendreau.'

'Do you think he'll file a complaint?'

'We'll also drop the charge of attempted murder, of which I was the victim.'

'Listen, Jules, you're on a losing streak. Don't waste your breath, it makes my heart ache. You're a good kid. Perhaps one day we'll bump into one another and have a couple of drinks. But here we're not on equal terms. You're as innocent as a choirboy. They'll make mincemeat out of you.'

'Who?'

'It doesn't matter! But let me tell you one thing: Bob was a decent fellow. He had his own ideas about how to behave in the world. He couldn't stand the sight of some people, but he was incapable of foul play. Get that clear.'

'He's dead.'

'He could be. I have no idea. Or, if I do know something, it's no one else's business. Now, I'm telling you as a friend, drop it!

147

'Do you get it? Drop it, Jules! I have nothing to say. I'll say nothing. You're out of your depth. Let's say we're both out of our depth.

'I know nothing, I saw nothing, I heard nothing. The fifty grand? I'll carry on repeating till the cows come home that I won it at the races.

'As for getting out of here, we'll see, won't we?'

And so saying, he gave a strange little smirk.

'Now, be a nice fellow and don't give poor Lucile a hard time. She really loved her Bob. Do you get that? A girl can be on the game and love her man. Don't torment her, and perhaps one day I'll thank you. That's all.'

He had stood up and of his own accord was heading for the door.

'Dédé!' called Maigret, also rising.

'That's it. I'm keeping mum. You won't get another word out of me.'

Dédé opened the door and called the officers.

'We're done,' he said with a leer.

The sergeant asked Maigret:

'Shall I bring you the woman?'

Lucile refused to sit down but insisted on standing in front of the desk.

'Do you know how Bob died?'

She sighed:

'I have no idea.'

'He was murdered in a house in Rue Chaptal.'

'Do you think so?'

'He was the lover of another girl.'

'I'm not jealous.'

'Why won't you talk?'

'Because I have nothing to say.'

'If you'd known that Bob was alive, you wouldn't have been on your way to Belgium.'

She clammed up.

'Why don't you want Bob to be avenged?'

She bit her lip and looked away.

'You prefer a fistful of money to seeing his killer put away?'

'You have no right to say that.'

'Then talk.'

'I don't know anything.'

'What if I helped you?'

'I wouldn't say anything.'

'Who have you seen since you've been here?'

At last Maigret understood. The reason he had been kept waiting was not because the inspector was busy. The Criminal Records department upstairs had been in touch with Quai des Orfèvres.

Had Dédé been photographed and his fingerprints taken? Had Lucile been given a medical examination? It was unlikely.

But it was almost certain that someone had questioned them, someone from the Sûreté.

By the time Maigret had arrived, at least an hour had elapsed since Le Bret had left Boulevard Richard-Lenoir.

It was hard to believe, and yet hadn't Dédé himself hinted that Maigret was being taken for a ride?

He left the room and had the feeling that they were laughing at him behind his back. The chief inspector returned just at that moment, as if by chance.

'Well, my friend? Success? Did they talk?'

'What are you planning to do with them?'

'I don't know yet. I'm awaiting orders.'

'From whom?'

'From on high, as usual.'

'Thank you.'

Maigret stepped into the street just as the skies opened. He felt so disillusioned that he was on the verge of handing in his notice.

'*You're as innocent as a choirboy*,' Dédé had said to him with a touch of pity.

He had so wanted to belong to this establishment, and now he was leaving demoralized, a feeling of disgust in the pit of his stomach.

He walked into the Brasserie Dauphine, where there were a few officers from Quai des Orfèvres having a drink. He knew them by sight, but for them he was a nobody.

First he took one of the pills the doctor had given him, in the hope that it would give him a boost, then he drank a large glass of spirits.

He saw them sitting around a table, looking rather unkempt, very much at ease. Those men were entitled to go anywhere, they knew everything, they exchanged information on the cases they were working on.

Did Maigret still want to be 'one of the boys'? Was he not beginning to discover that his idea of the police was completely mistaken?

After the second glass, he was on the point of going to see his protector, the big boss, Xavier Guichard, to tell him what was on his mind.

They had made a fool of him. When Le Bret had come to visit him, he'd wormed information out of him. His car was waiting at the door. Most likely he'd told the driver to go straight to Quai des Orfèvres, where he would certainly not have been kept waiting.

'My secretary is over-zealous. He's going to put his foot in it and bring us trouble.'

Who knows whether he went to his superiors, to the commissioner, for example, or even the minister of the interior?

Perhaps the minister of the interior was also a regular dinner guest at Rue Chaptal?

By now Maigret was convinced they had only allowed him to handle the case — warning him to be cautious — so that he would fall at the first hurdle.

*You want to question Dédé? Why not? Go ahead, my boy.*

Only beforehand, they'd had a word with the garage owner. Who knows what they'd promised him in exchange for keeping his mouth shut. It was easy. This wasn't the first time he'd been in trouble. As for Lucile, if she didn't keep quiet, they could always put her away for a spell in Saint-Lazare.

*You're as innocent as a choirboy.*

He laughed nervously, because he really had been a choirboy back in his village.

Everything had been tainted. *His* police force was tainted. He wasn't just vexed that he had been robbed of his little success. It was something deeper; he felt more like a jilted lover.

'Waiter!'

He almost ordered a third drink, changed his mind, paid, and left with the feeling that the four others at their table were laughing at him behind his back.

He realized that from now on everything would be rigged. What could he do? Go and find the flautist. Justin Minard was his only trump card: a flautist! It was because of him that Le Bret had launched an investigation in the first place.

If Maigret got angry, they would claim that the blow to his head had affected his mind.

He clambered on to a passing omnibus and stood sullenly on the platform, breathing in the wet-dog smell coming from his overcoat. He felt hot. Was he perhaps running a slight temperature?

On reaching Rue Chaptal, he nearly turned back at the thought of Paumelle, the owner of the Vieux Calvados, who had been so patronizing towards him.

Perhaps they were right after all? Perhaps he'd been mistaken, and wasn't made of the right stuff for a career in the police?

And yet he was so certain of what he would have done had he had a free hand! He would have searched every nook and cranny of that house, which he could see from the street. He would also have got to know the people who lived there. He would have discovered all their secrets, starting with the late elderly Balthazar and finishing with Lise Gendreau and Louis.

The main thing was not to find out precisely what had happened on the night of the 15th – that was only an end. It would be easy to piece together their comings and goings once he knew each person's inner thoughts.

But the house was a stronghold whose gates were closed to him, just like the one on Avenue du Bois. People came racing to the rescue at the slightest alert. Dédé had suddenly clammed up and Lucile was resisting the urge to avenge her Bob.

He realized that he had been talking to himself as he walked. He shrugged and flung open the door of the little restaurant.

Justin was there, standing at the bar, holding a glass. He had taken Maigret's place and was chatting to Paumelle, who showed no surprise at the sight of the newcomer.

'The same for me,' Maigret ordered.

The main door was wide open. The downpour was petering out and there was sunshine between the raindrops. The glistening pavement would be dry in no time.

'I thought you'd be back,' said Paumelle. 'What baffles me is that you're not with the other gentlemen.'

Maigret wheeled round to look at Justin Minard, who hesitated. Eventually, he said:

'There are a lot of people in the house. They arrived around half an hour ago.'

There were no cars in the street. The visitors had probably arrived in cabs.

'Who are they?'

'I don't know them. It looks like a raid by the prosecutor's office. There's a gentleman with a white beard, accompanied by a young man, maybe the prosecutor and his clerk?'

Clenching his glass, Maigret asked:

'Then what?'

'People I've never seen.'

Justin tactfully did not say what he thought, and it was Paumelle who grumbled:

'Colleagues of yours. Not from the local police station. From Quai des Orfèvres. I recognized one of them.'

Poor Minard! He didn't know where to look. He too felt as if he had been duped. Maigret had let him think that he was in charge of the case and the flautist had thrown himself body and soul into helping him.

And now it transpired that Maigret was a nobody and that he wasn't even being kept abreast of developments.

Once again, Maigret was tempted to go home to write his furious letter of resignation then retire to bed. His head was burning and hurting with a stabbing pain. The owner was brandishing a bottle of calvados in mid-air, and Maigret nodded.

Too bad! He'd been made a fool of from the start. They were right. He was an innocent.

'Germaine is in the house,' muttered Minard. 'I spotted her at a window.'

Naturally! Her too. She might not be very bright, but she had a certain intuition, like all women. She had realized that she had chosen the wrong side, that Maigret and his flautist were just pawns.

'I'm going over there!' Maigret suddenly decided, putting his glass down on the bar.

He was so afraid that his courage would fail him that he rushed across the road. From the archway, he saw two men digging in a corner of the garden. To the left, in front of the main door into the hall, a police officer stood guard.

'I'm from the local police station,' said Maigret.

'You'll have to wait.'

'Wait for what?'

'For these gentlemen to finish.'

'But I'm in charge of this case.'

'Maybe, but I have my orders.'

Another one from Quai des Orfèvres!

'If ever I work for the Sûreté,' Maigret promised himself, already forgetting his firm resolve to leave the police, 'I swear I'll never show contempt for the poor fellows from the local police stations.'

'The prosecutor?'

'All those gentlemen.'

'Is the chief with them?'

'I don't know him. What does he look like?'

'He's wearing a grey tailcoat. He's tall and thin, with a blond pencil moustache.'

'Haven't seen him.'

'Who's here from Quai des Orfèvres?'

'Detective Chief Inspector Barodet.'

His name was forever appearing in the newspapers. In Maigret's eyes, he was perhaps the most distinguished man in the world, with his clean-shaven face that made him look like a butler, and prying, beady little eyes that always seemed to be looking elsewhere.

'The body?'

The police officer was reluctant to reply to Maigret's questions, and did so condescendingly.

'Is Richard Gendreau in the house?'

'What does he look like?'

'Dark hair and a long, crooked nose.'

'He is.'

So, either Gendreau hadn't gone to his office as usual, or he had hurried back.

Just then, a cab drew up outside. A young woman alighted and hurried towards the door where the two men stood talking.

She couldn't have seen Maigret.

'Mademoiselle Gendreau,' she said tentatively.

And the officer opened the door to her at once, saying to Maigret:

'I had orders.'

'Were they expecting her?'

'I was simply told to let her in.'

'Have you seen the butler?'

'He's with the gentlemen from Quai des Orfèvres right now. Are you familiar with the case?'

'A little,' replied Maigret, swallowing his pride.

'Apparently he was a nasty piece of work.'

'Who?'

'The fellow who was shot by the servant.'

Maigret stared at him, open-mouthed.

'Are you certain?'

'Of what?'

'That Louis . . .'

'Look, I don't even know who Louis is. I just overheard snatches of conversation. What I do know is that it's best to avoid attracting a crowd.'

One of the men who was digging and who was definitely a police officer entered the porch; the one who remained in the garden must be the manservant. The officer had mud on his hands and on his shoes, and wore an expression of disgust.

'He's not a pretty sight!' he said in passing.

A door opened and he vanished into the house. In the split second the door was ajar, Maigret caught a glimpse of Lise Gendreau and her brother who stood talking in the entrance hall. The men from the prosecutor's office must be in one of the drawing rooms behind closed doors.

'Do you have an appointment?' the police officer asked Maigret, whose impatience was visible.

'I don't know.'

It was enough to make him cry. Never had he been so humiliated.

'I think they're more afraid of the press than anyone else. That's why they're taking so many precautions. The funny thing is that at home we drink Balthazar coffee. I had no idea that one day . . .'

They must be making a lot of telephone calls in the house, for they could hear frequent clicks and ringing.

'If your chief inspector sent you, I can go and tell them that you're out here waiting.'

'There's no point.'

The officer shrugged. He didn't understand what Maigret meant, and watched him take a pill.

'Are you not well?'

'Do you have any idea how it all started?'

'How what started?'

'Were you at Quai des Orfèvres?'

'Yes, I was just off on a stake-out in La Villette. Chief Inspector Barodet was giving a guy a roasting.'

'A short fellow in a check suit?'

'Yes, a brash fellow.'

'Did someone telephone the inspector?'

'No. The chief called him in. While he was gone, he asked me to keep an eye on the fellow. A funny one. He asked me for a cigarette, but I didn't have any.'

'Then what?'

'When Monsieur Barodet came back, he shut himself away with the fellow in the check suit for a moment, after telling us to be at the ready.'

'Who?'

'The men in the squad. There are three of us here, plus the chief inspector. The other two are inside. The one who was digging, that's Barrère. He got a bullet in his body a month ago as he was arresting the Pole of Rue Caulaincourt.'

Every word was loaded. Maigret pictured the inspectors' office, the amiable authority of Barodet who called them 'my boys'.

Why had they done this to him? Had he made a mistake? Had he gone about things the wrong way? Had he not been of the utmost discretion?

When Chief Inspector Le Bret had visited Maigret's apartment on Boulevard Richard-Lenoir, he seemed to be giving him carte blanche. But then Le Bret had raced over to Quai des Orfèvres! Then perhaps he'd come here?

'So the butler admits he did it?'

'That's my understanding. He looks like a thug, at any rate.'

'I'm at a loss to understand.'

'Because you like to think you can understand?'

It was perhaps Maigret's first true lesson in modesty. The police officer was older than him. He was over thirty. He had the calm air, the sort of indifference of those who have seen many things. He puffed gently on his pipe without craning to hear what was being said inside.

'It's still better than hiding out for hours on end in some alley in La Villette.'

Now a car was pulling up outside the house. A young doctor with a dark beard jumped out clutching his bag, and Maigret recognized him from the photographs in the newspapers. He was Doctor Paul, the coroner, who was already quite famous.

'Where are the gentlemen from headquarters?'

'This way, doctor. The body is in the garden, but I presume you would like to see the prosecutor first?'

They all went into the inner sanctum, apart from Maigret, who was left to champ at the bit under the arch.

'You'll see,' said the officer, 'there will only be three lines in the papers about it.'

'Why?'

'Because!'

And true enough, that evening, there was a paragraph in *La Presse* saying:

*During the night of the 15th of this month, a burglar broke into the private residence of the Gendreau-Balthazar family in Rue*

*Chaptal. The butler, Louis Viaud, aged fifty-six, born in Anseval, Nièvre, killed him with a bullet to the chest.*

That night, Maigret was lying in bed with a temperature of thirty-nine, while Madame Maigret wondered how to get rid of the flautist, who refused to leave the room and seemed more like a lost dog than ever.

# 9. Lunch in the Country

It lasted three days. At first he'd hoped that he would really be ill, and that would infuriate *them*. But on the first morning, when he cautiously opened his eyes, the only thing wrong with him seemed to be a nasty cold in the head.

So he was shamming, trying to fool even his wife. It was ridiculous to have nothing more serious than a cold in the head, so he groaned, coughed and complained of chest pains.

'I'm going to give you a mustard poultice, Jules. That will stop you getting bronchitis.'

Madame Maigret was as cheerful as ever. She nursed him tenderly. You could say she pampered him. And yet he had the feeling that she wasn't taken in.

'Come in, Monsieur Minard,' he heard her saying in the adjacent room. 'No, he's no worse. Only please don't tire him out.'

That meant that she was playing along.

'His temperature?' asked the flautist anxiously.

'No cause for concern.'

And she took care not to say what it was, because if anything it was subnormal.

She loved concocting herbal teas and poultices and making broth or egg custard. She also liked to draw the curtains gently and walk around on tiptoe, half-open the door sometimes and peek in to make sure he was asleep.

Poor Minard had already become a nuisance! Maigret was annoyed with himself. He was fond of the flautist and wished he could be kind to him.

He would turn up at around nine or ten in the morning. He didn't ring the bell but discreetly scratched at the door in case Maigret had fallen asleep. Then he would whisper, come into the room brushing the doorpost, and walk over to the bed.

'No, don't move. I've simply come to find out how you are. Do you need me to do anything? I'd be so happy to help you out!'

It was no longer a matter of playing detective. Anything to help. He also offered Madame Maigret his services.

'Why don't you let me go to the market for you? I'm very good at shopping, you know.'

He ended up perching by the window for a moment, on one buttock, and would stay for hours. If they asked after his wife, he answered sharply:

'It doesn't matter.'

He came back in the late afternoon, in evening dress on his way to work. Now he was playing in a dance hall on Boulevard Saint-Michel, no longer the double bass but the cornet, which must be hard for him. It left a pink ring in the centre of his lips.

Every morning Le Bret also sent over an orderly from the police station for news. The concierge had been disappointed. She knew that her tenant was an official, but he had never told her that he was a police officer.

'The chief inspector says to take good care of yourself, and not to worry. Everything's fine.'

He snuggled under the covers of his damp bed, which smelled strongly of sweat. It was a way of withdrawing into himself. He didn't know yet that this would become a quirk, that he would often resort to this behaviour in his moments of despondency or confusion.

The shift happened almost to order. Instead of his ideas becoming clear, they became scrambled, as they do when a person is feverish. He slipped gently into a half-sleep, and reality took on new forms, merging with childhood memories; the light and shadows of the room also played a part, and even the flowers on the wallpaper, the aromas from the kitchen and Madame Maigret's muffled footsteps.

He always went back to the same point, picking up his characters like chess pieces, old Balthazar, the Gendreaus, the father, Lise and Richard, the Chateau d'Anseval, Louis, Germaine, the little maid, Marie.

He moved them around, distorted them. Then came the turn of Le Bret leaving the Maigrets' apartment on Boulevard Richard-Lenoir, getting into his gig and saying to his coachman: 'Quai des Orfèvres.'

Was he on first-name terms with the big chief, Xavier Guichard? This was where it became harrowing. What was Le Bret saying to him, in the vast office which Maigret had been inside twice and which he thought was the most awe-inspiring place in the world?

'My secretary, that young man you recommended to me, is handling a case. I had no alternative but to give it to him. But I fear he's going to put his foot in it.'

Was that what he was saying? Possibly. Above all, Le Bret was a man of the world. He fenced every morning at the

Hoche club, frequented the salons, attended all the premières and appeared at the races in a light grey top hat.

But what about Xavier Guichard? He'd been a friend of Maigret's father and was from the same social class. He didn't live in the exclusive Monceau district but in a little apartment in the Latin Quarter surrounded by his books rather than by beautiful women.

No, he wasn't capable of playing a dirty trick or of compromise!

And yet, he had called Barodet. What orders had he given him?

And if that were true, did that mean that Maigret was wrong? He hadn't concluded his investigation, granted. He didn't know who had shot the count. Nor did he know why. But he would have got to the bottom of it.

He was conscious of having done a good job in a very short time. As was proved by the fact that Le Bret had been alarmed.

So why had he been?

There was no more mention of the case in the newspapers. It had been hushed up. Bob's body must have been taken to the morgue for the autopsy.

He saw himself back in the courtyard in Rue Chaptal, behind the others, the high-ups who ignored him. Barodet, who didn't know him personally, must have taken him for one of the servants. The prosecutor, the examining magistrate and the clerk of the court thought he was one of Barodet's men.

Only Louis had shot him a smug look. He had probably been told of Maigret's activities by Germaine.

All that was humiliating, discouraging. There were moments when, his eyes closed, his body clammy, he formed a plan for the perfect investigation.

'Next time, I'll go about it like this . . .'

Then, abruptly, on the fourth morning, he'd had enough of being ill and, before the arrival of the flautist, he got up, had a thorough wash, carefully shaved, and removed the dressing from his head.

'Are you going to the office?'

He wanted to get back to the smell of the police station, his black desk and the seedy-looking customers on their bench against the white wall.

'What should I tell Justin?'

Now they called him Justin, like a family friend or kinsman.

'If he wants to come and meet me at one o'clock, we can have lunch together.'

He hadn't slept with his moustache net on and he had to straighten the tips with a hot curling iron. He walked most of the way, to soak up the atmosphere of the boulevards, and his resentment melted away in the spring sunshine.

'What's the point of my worrying about those people?'

The Gendreaus in their stronghold. The old man's character that was passed on through the female line. Their battles over the will. The question of who would inherit the Balthazar Coffee empire . . .

Because it dawned on him that this wasn't just about money. Once people have a considerable fortune, it is no longer money that matters but power.

It was about deciding who would have the biggest pile

of shares, who would be chairman of the board. Lise or Richard?

It had to be deeply ingrained for a young woman to forget her twenty-one years and only think of taking up the director's role, as her mother had done before her.

To be the big boss!

'Let them fight it out between them!'

That was it! That was exactly what they had done. And a man had been killed, who nobody grieved for except for a girl who walked the streets around Avenue de Wagram.

He went into the police station and shook hands with his colleagues.

'Bertrand has gone over to your place to find out how you are.'

He didn't let Le Bret know he was there but went and sat at his desk without a word. It wasn't until ten thirty that on half-opening the baize door his boss spotted him.

'Are you here, Maigret? Come in and see me.'

He was trying to sound offhand.

'Have a seat. I wonder whether you're doing the right thing in coming back to work so soon. I was planning to offer you convalescence leave. Don't you think that a few days in the country would do you good?'

'I feel perfectly fit.'

'Good! Good! By the way, as you'll have seen, this whole business is resolved now. And I congratulate you, for actually you weren't so far from the truth. On the same day that I visited you, Louis telephoned the police.'

'Of his own accord?'

'I really have no idea. Besides, it makes no difference. The main thing is that he confessed to the crime. He must have got wind of your investigation and realized that you would uncover the truth.'

Maigret stared fixedly at the desk, and his face showed no emotion. Ill at ease, Le Bret continued:

'He went over our heads and contacted the Préfecture directly. Have you read the papers?'

'Yes.'

'Naturally the truth has been slightly rearranged. Sometimes it's a necessity, as you will understand one day. There are cases where there's no point creating a scandal, where the harsh truth does more harm than good. Let me explain. We both know that the count didn't break into the house as a burglar. Perhaps he was expected? Lise Gendreau was very nice to him. I use the word in the best sense.

'Don't forget that she was born at the Chateau d'Anseval and that there are ties between her family and his.

'Bob was a hothead. He was on a downward spiral. Why would she not have tried to help him back on to the straight and narrow?

'That's the opinion of my wife, who knows her well.

'Anyway, it's of little importance. Was he drunk that night, as he often was? Did he behave in a scandalous manner?

'Louis gave few details. He heard screams. When he entered the room, Bob and Richard Gendreau were fighting and he thought he saw the gleam of a knife in the count's hand.'

'Has the knife been found?' Maigret asked quietly without looking up.

He seemed to be gazing obstinately at a little stain on the mahogany desk.

'I don't know. It's Barodet who questioned him. The fact remains that there was a pistol on the bedside table and that Louis, fearing for his master's life, fired it.

'Now, my young friend, tell me who would have benefited from a scandal? The public wouldn't have accepted the truth. We live in times when certain social classes are constantly being targeted. Mademoiselle Gendreau's honour was at stake, because it is her reputation that would have suffered.

'In any case, we are dealing with a case of self-defence.'

'Are you certain that it was the butler who fired?'

'We have his confession. Think about it, Maigret. Ask yourself how a certain section of the press would have reacted, and what the repercussions would have been for the young woman who can be accused of nothing other than imprudence.'

'I understand.'

'Mademoiselle Gendreau has left for Switzerland. Her nerves are shattered, and she will probably rest for a few months. Louis has been released and it is likely that the case will be dismissed. His only crime was to have panicked and buried the body in the garden instead of owning up immediately.'

'Did he do it alone?'

'Put yourself in Richard Gendreau's position. I see that you don't yet understand, but you will. There are cases where we have no right . . .'

And, while he struggled to find the right words, Maigret looked up and said in a neutral, almost naive tone:

'To do as our conscience dictates?'

Then, abruptly, Le Bret became curt again, loftier than ever.

'My conscience is clear,' he snapped, 'and I would claim that it is as sensitive as anyone else's. You are young, Maigret, very young, and that is the only reason why I can't hold it against you.'

It was midday when the telephone rang in the big main office. Inspector Besson, who had picked it up, shouted:

'For you, Maigret. It's that fellow who's already called three times. Always at the same time.'

Maigret grabbed the receiver.

'Hello! Jules?'

He recognized Dédé's voice.

'Are you feeling better? Are you back at work? Tell me, are you free for lunch?'

'Why?'

'A little idea of mine. Ever since the other night, I've been wanting to take you to lunch in the country. Don't be scared. I'll come and pick you up in the car. Not outside the police station, because I'm not very fond of those places, but on the corner of Rue Fontaine. All right?'

Poor old Justin Minard was going to be left high and dry once again.

'Tell him that I had to go out on important business, that I'll see him tonight or tomorrow.'

A quarter of an hour later, he clambered into the grey De Dion-Bouton. Dédé was alone.

'What do you fancy? Do you like fried gudgeon? First we're going to stop at Porte Maillot for a quick drink.'

They went into a bar, and Dédé ordered two stiff absinthes, letting the water to drip on to the sugar lump balanced on the perforated spoon and watching it slowly dissolve.

He was cheerful, with a hint of earnestness in his expression. He was wearing a check suit, greenish-yellow shoes and a splendid red tie.

'Another? No? As you wish. I have no reason to get you drunk this time.'

Then it was back on the road, the banks of the Seine, with fishermen in their boats, and finally a little riverside inn with leafy arbours dotted around the garden.

'A slap-up meal, Gustave. For starters, fried fish, only gudgeon.'

And to Maigret:

'He's going to net some for us and cook them live.'

Then to the owner:

'What will you serve us for the main course?'

'A coq au vin made with a Beaujolais rosé?'

'Let's go for the coq au vin.'

Dédé was very much at home here. He sniffed around in the kitchen and went down to the cellar, returning with a bottle of white Loire wine.

'It's better than all the aperitifs in the world. Now, while we're waiting for our fish, fill your pipe. We can talk.'

He had an urge to explain:

'I insisted on seeing you because deep down I like you. You're not corrupt yet, like most of the boys in your outfit.'

He too embroidered the truth a little, Maigret knew. People of Dédé's sort are blabbermouths, and that's often how they get caught. They're so proud of themselves that they can't resist the desire to boast.

'Where's Lucile?' asked Maigret, who had expected her to be with them.

'She really is ill, believe it or not. That girl really was mad about Bob, you see. She'd have put her head on the block for him. She was completely devastated. First of all, she wouldn't leave Rue Brey, saying that every step would remind her of him. Yesterday, I persuaded her to go away to the country. I drove her there and I'll go and pick her up again. But enough! Maybe we'll talk about her later.'

He lit a cigarette and blew the smoke out slowly through his nostrils. The wine sparkled in the glasses, the breeze made the young leaves of the bower quiver. They could see the owner standing in his skiff, peering into the water before casting his net.

'I presume you were curious enough to have a look at my file and that you will have seen that I never take risks. Little jobs, yes. Twice I copped six months and I swore that that was enough.'

He drank to keep up his spirits.

'Have you read the papers?'

And when Maigret nodded:

'Clever, very clever, that lot. You should have seen Lucile! She turned as white as a ghost. She was determined to go and find them and squawk. I calmed her down. I kept saying to her: "What would be the point?"'

'They sullied his name all right, didn't they? I swear to you, if I could get the guy with the broken nose – Richard,

171

his name is – in a corner where there are no cops, I'd happily smash his face in.

'He coughed up fifty grand and he thinks that's the end of it. Well! Between you and me – even though you're a cop – I tell you that's not the end of it. We'll meet again one day, sooner or later. There are bastards and bastards. That type of bastard, I can't stand.

'What about you?'

'I was taken off the case,' mumbled Maigret.

'I know. I'm paid to know.'

'Did they order you to keep quiet?'

'They told me that all I needed to do was keep mum and I'd have my "deal".'

Which meant that the police would turn a blind eye to Dédé's peccadilloes, they'd forget the blow to Maigret's head and they wouldn't investigate where the 49,000 francs found in his wallet had come from.

'What bowled me over was the butler's story. Do *you* believe that?'

'No.'

'Right! Otherwise you'd have gone down in my esteem. Since someone had to have pulled the trigger, it might as well be the servant. Who do you reckon fired the shot? We can talk here, can't we? Mind you, if you try and use what I've told you, I'll swear I kept my mouth shut. I think it was the girl.'

'So do I . . .'

'The difference being that I have good reason to believe so. I'd also add that if she shot Bob, it was by mistake. It was the brother she was trying to kill. Because those two loathe each other the way people in those families do.

'It's a pity you never met Bob. He was the most decent fellow on earth. Boy, he could drive them all round the bend!

'But not out of spite. He didn't have a mean bone in his body. It was something else. He despised them so much that he found them laughable.

'When the girl started hanging around him—'

'How long ago?'

'It was last autumn. I don't know who told her. Everyone knew that after the races, at around five thirty, you could always find Bob in a bar in Avenue de Wagram.'

'She went there.'

'She did too! And without a veil. She told him who she was, that she lived at the Chateau d'Anseval, that she was interested in him and he'd be welcome to visit her at her house.'

'Did he sleep with her?'

'You can say that again! He even took her to the hotel in Rue Brey that you've been to. To see how far she'd go, you know? He was a good-looking kid. But she wasn't the kind of doll to go into a hotel like that just for the pleasure of being screwed.

'Besides, she had no more feelings than a brick wall. He didn't keep it secret for Lucile's sake. If she was going to be jealous of all the girls that passed through his hands! Ah, here's the fish. Tell me how you find it.'

He could eat and talk at the same time and he continued to indulge in both, caressing the second bottle that had been placed in front of them.

'Don't try to understand. It took Bob himself a while to see clearly and – no offence – he was cleverer than the two of us put together. What surprised him the most was that she wanted to marry him.

'She offered him a deal. He would no longer need to work and would receive an allowance every month for his day-to-day expenses and everything. He strung her along. He said to himself that she was desperate to be called the Countess d'Anseval. There are people like that. They buy themselves a chateau, then they want a title, to buy a set of ancestors. That's what Bob explained to me.'

He looked Maigret in the eye and announced, pleased at catching him off-balance:

'Well, that wasn't it.'

He crunched the crisp gudgeon, glancing from time to time at the Seine, where barges glided slowly past, sounding their sirens as they approached the lock.

'Don't try, you'll never guess. When Bob found out, he was staggered. And yet he knew the family history inside out. Do you know whose idea the marriage was? The old man's!'

He was triumphant.

'Admit that it was worth coming out to Bougival for lunch. You've heard about the shrivelled-up old boy who wanted to leave his house and his paintings to the state to be turned into a museum? If you want a laugh, listen to what comes next. I don't know the full story, mind you. Neither did Bob. Apparently, the old boy, who had started out as a country pedlar, dreamed of having grandchildren of true noble blood.

'Do you want to know what I think? That for him it was a sort of revenge. Because it appears that the Ansevals weren't very nice to him. They sold him the chateau and the farms. Then they discreetly withdrew. They wouldn't once invite him to dinner, or even to lunch.

'So he put clauses in his will that riled the entire family.

'His daughter was still alive when he died, but those people with their millions plan a long way ahead.

'On the death of the daughter, the shares were to be split between two parties: 51 per cent for the young lady and 49 per cent for crooked-nose. Apparently, it was very important that the majority vote as they call it went to the young lady.

'Me, I don't know much about these things. Anyway. It was to happen when she turned twenty-one.'

'Next month,' said Maigret.

'I'll have some more. Too bad if I'm too full for the coq au vin. Where were we? Right! Only there was another little problem. If the young lady married an Anseval, then she would receive *all* the shares, and it would be left to her discretion to give her brother an allowance equivalent to his holding.

'That means that he would no longer have had anything to do with the coffee company, the chateau, etc. The Balthazars and the Gendreaus would have become Ansevals, their lineage going back to the Crusades.

'Bob was well up on these things, and you have no idea how it made him laugh.'

'Did he agree to the deal?'

'What do you take him for?'

'How did he find out?'

'Through the brother. And you'll see how a man can stupidly lose his life. The Gendreau with a broken nose is no fool. He doesn't want to end up like his father, spending all his time in clubs and chasing errand girls in Rue de la Paix. He wants to be the boss too.'

'I'm beginning to see.'

'No, you can't possibly see, because Bob didn't see at first. Richard asked him to come to his office. Apparently it's like a sacristy, with carved wood on the walls, gothic furniture, a floor-to-ceiling portrait of the old man who seems to be laughing at you.

'To be honest, out of the lot of them, that old man is still the one I'd find easiest to get on with. Bob used to say that he was the most mischievous devil he'd ever come across. So to speak, because he was dead. Anyhow . . .

'So the brother comes out with his spiel. He asks Bob if he's decided whether to marry his sister. Bob replies that he never had any intention of doing so.

'The brother tells him that he's making a mistake, that it would be a good deal for everyone.

'And why would it be a good deal? Because he, Richard Gendreau, would hand over a pile of dough to his sister's husband. As much dough as he wanted. On the sole condition that he promise to show his sister a good time, entertain her, and get her to give up her love of business.

'Do you see now?

'Bob replied that he didn't feel cut out for that job.

'So the bastard with the crooked nose declared that that was just too bad for him, that he would end up paying a high price.

'When I think that you'd have had me thrown in jail for having got that fellow to cough up fifty thousand! I don't hold it against you. You couldn't have known.'

Now they basked in a wonderful aroma of coq au vin and despite what Dédé had said earlier, he still had a healthy appetite.

'Try this Beaujolais and admit that it would have been a pity to deprive me of such a feast and put me on a diet of beans.

'Do you know what he had in his bag, that idiot? I said that Bob was a decent guy but I didn't claim he was a saint. It happened – as it does to everyone – that he found himself a bit short. All his life he'd known loads of swanky people. So sometimes, for a laugh, he'd imitate their signature on banker's drafts or other bank forms.

'He didn't mean any harm. The proof is that no one ever filed a complaint, and things always worked out in the end.

'Well, Jules, the idiot had got hold of a whole pile of those forms from God knows where.

'"*If you don't marry my sister, I'll have you locked up. If, when you have married her, you don't toe the line, I'll have you locked up.*"

'Harsh! Even harsher than the old man!

'I swear Bob was sorry he got mixed up with the girl and that whole business.

'Meanwhile, the young lady was in a hurry. She wanted the wedding right away, before she turned twenty-one. She sent him letters by pneumatic tube, dispatches. She arranged to meet him time and time again.

'Sometimes he came, sometimes he didn't, and she'd turn up in Rue Brey looking for him. She'd wait on the corner of the avenue not caring whether she was mistaken for something else.

'Lucile knew her well.'

'When you drove Bob to Rue Chaptal, on the night of the 15th—'

'He'd decided to finish it, to come clean and tell her that he would not be bought, either by her or by her brother.'

'Did he ask you to wait for him?'

'Not exactly, but he didn't expect to be long. Breast or leg? You should have more mushrooms. Gustave picks them himself and preserves them.'

Maigret felt perfectly relaxed, possibly thanks to the Beaujolais on top of the dry white wine.

'You're wondering why I'm telling you all this?'

'No.'

'You know?'

'Yes.'

Or at least he intuited it. Dédé needed to get it off his chest – or spit it out, as he would have said – and could no longer keep quiet. Here there was no danger. Besides, he had his 'deal'.

But he wasn't proud of that. This lunch was a way for him to salve his conscience. Revealing others' dirty doings made him appear in a relatively virtuous light.

Maigret would remember that lunch at Bougival for a long time to come, and that memory possibly helped him avoid making rash judgements.

'I know nothing about what happened up there.'

Neither did Maigret, but it was already becoming easier to reconstruct. What they needed to know was whether

Richard Gendreau was supposed to be in the house. Perhaps, that night, he should have been at his club, or elsewhere?

And again, perhaps – and it was in his nature – it was Bob himself who had asked him to go upstairs? Why not?

In order to tell the pair of them what he thought of their scheming.

'First of all, I'm not getting married.'

Maigret, who had never seen him, was beginning to have a sense of his character and even of his appearance.

'I have no desire to sell a name that I don't even bother to use.'

Because although around Place des Ternes and on the race-courses some called him the count, most of his acquaintances were convinced it was a nickname and were unaware of his real name.

Did Lise Gendreau throw a tantrum and talk about her reputation? Did her brother lose his temper?

'And you can shut up! Besides, I'm going to tell your little sister about the little deal you cooked up.'

Did he have the chance? Or did Richard go for him straight away?

Hundreds of thousands of people who drank Balthazar coffee and stuck flower cards in albums, like Madame Maigret, had no idea that their morning coffee had been at stake in the bedroom battle in Rue Chaptal.

A vicious battle, which a servant listening at the keyhole had probably overheard.

The two men must have grabbed hold of each other. Perhaps they had rolled on the floor.

Was Richard Gendreau armed? He was definitely the sort to stab someone in the back.

'I reckon it was the bitch that killed him. Not intentionally. She genuinely panicked. The proof is that the first thing she did, which she must later have regretted, was to open the window and call for help. Unless the window was open? I must say I hadn't looked.

'You see, I wonder whether she hadn't ended up being truly in love with Bob. These things happen. She began because it suited her purpose. Then she fell for him. Not physically, I've already told you that she's made of wood. But he was so different from the fossils she was used to meeting . . .

'I reckon that when she saw that Bob had the upper hand, or that her brother was trying to do the dirty on her, she lost her head. She fired. Unfortunately, she's a lousy shot and it was Bob she hit in the belly. Shall we ask for another bottle? This little wine's not bad for two sous. So there you have it, Jules my friend!

'When I saw the guy hammering on the door to be let in, I skedaddled, then I came back, but there was nothing more to be seen. I decided to make myself scarce.

'We thought about it, Lucile and me. We still hoped that Bob would come back, or that we'd hear he was in hospital.

'In the end I went to see Gendreau in his office. That's how I know what the old man looked like.

'Would it have been better if no one had profited from this?

'He coughed up almost immediately, and I wished I'd asked for a hundred grand instead of fifty.

'Bunch of crooks!

'You turned up just as we were about to scram. It would have been too dumb to get caught, you've got to admit.

'Cheers, my friend!'

'They settled things in their own way. I'm beginning to get used to it. It makes me sick every time I see one of their delivery vehicles with their neatly harnessed horses and a well-groomed coachman in the driver's seat.

'*Patron!* Coffee, but not Balthazar.'

But there was no other choice.

'That's annoying!' he grumbled under his breath. 'I'm glad we're going to live in the country.'

'You and Lucile?'

'She didn't say no. We've got fifty thousand, or near enough. I've always dreamed of running a little restaurant by the river, something like this, with customers who are pals. It's hard to find a place, because it would need to be not too far from a race-course. Tomorrow, I'm going to hunt around Maisons-Laffitte. That's where I've taken Lucile.'

He looked a little sheepish and added hastily:

'Don't you go thinking that we've become law-abiding!'

It lasted for a week. Each morning, the bell summoned Maigret into the chief inspector's office, where he presented his daily reports. Each morning, Le Bret opened his mouth as if he were about to say something, and then looked away.

They did not exchange a word other than for strictly office matters. Maigret was more earnest than before, as if heavier, even though he had not yet put on weight. He didn't bother to smile, and he was perfectly conscious that for Le Bret he was like a living rebuke.

'Tell me, my boy . . .'

That was in early May.

'When are you due to take your exam?'

The famous course he had been studying for the night the flautist had burst into his office, into his life.

'Next week.'

'Do you expect to pass?'

'I hope so.'

He remained cool, almost terse.

'Guichard tells me that your ambition was to work at Quai des Orfèvres.'

'Yes, sir.'

'Is it no longer so?'

'I don't know.'

'I think you would be more at home there and, even though you are invaluable to me here, I think I'm going to intercede to have you transferred.'

Maigret, a lump in his throat, didn't breathe a word. He was sulking. Deep down, he still resented them, all of them, his boss, the Gendreaus, the men from the Sûreté, perhaps even Guichard, who was a father figure for him.

But if Guichard . . .

It was inevitably they who were right, he vaguely realized. A scandal would have been pointless. In any case, Lise Gendreau would have been acquitted.

'Well?'

Was it not life itself that he was angry at, and was it not he who was in the wrong not to understand it?

He had no intention of being bought. He refused to be indebted in any way to Chief Inspector Le Bret.

'I'll wait my turn,' he managed to mutter.

The very next day, he was summoned to Quai des Orfèvres.

'Still angry, my boy?' asked the big chief, clapping him on the shoulder.

He couldn't help blurting out, almost furiously, like a child: 'It was Lise Gendreau who killed Bob.'

'Probably.'

'You knew?'

'I suspected as much. If it had been her brother, Louis wouldn't have sacrificed himself.'

The windows were open on to the Seine. Tugs trailing their strings of barges sounded their sirens before passing under the bridge and lowering their funnels. A constant stream of trams, omnibuses, carriages and taxis crossed Pont Saint-Michel, and the streets were alive with women in pastel frocks.

'Have a seat, my friend.'

The lesson he learned that day, given in a paternal voice, wasn't in his technical police manuals.

'Try to do as little damage as possible. Do you understand? What would it have achieved?'

'The truth.'

'What truth?'

And the big chief concluded:

'You can re-light your pipe. On Monday you will start here as an inspector under Detective Chief Inspector Barodet.'

Maigret did not yet know that one day, twenty-two years later, he would come across Lise again, under a different name, an aristocratic Italian name, that of her husband.

Or that she would receive him in the unchanged office

of Balthazar Coffee which he had only heard about from a certain Dédé — where he would finally see the portrait of the old man, still gracing the wall.

'Inspector . . .'

That was *him*.

'I don't need to ask you to exercise discretion . . .'

By that time, the Sûreté had changed its name to the Police Judiciaire.

And it handled 'Investigations undertaken on behalf of private families', as they were called in official jargon.

'Unfortunately my daughter has her father's character.'

She on the other hand was cool and calm, like old Balthazar, whose full-length portrait hung behind her chair.

'She allowed herself to become involved with an unscrupulous individual who has taken her to England, where he obtained a marriage licence. They must not, *at all costs . . .*'

No, he did not yet know that, once again, the honour of the Balthazars would be in his hands.

He was twenty-six years old. He couldn't wait to go and tell his wife the news:

'I'm being transferred to the chief's squad.'

But he couldn't do so straight away. Justin Minard was waiting for him in the street.

'Bad news?'

'Good news. I've been promoted.'

The flautist looked more excited than he did.

'Are you leaving the police station?'

'As of tomorrow.'

'Shall we celebrate?'

At the Brasserie Dauphine, a stone's throw from Quai

des Orfèvres, inspectors from headquarters were having a drink, taking no notice of the two men celebrating over a bottle of sparkling wine.

In a few days' time, they would know at least one of them. Maigret would be their equal. He would be at home in this café, the waiter would greet him by his name and know what his favourite drink was.

When he got home that evening he was drunk. Ten times he and Justin Minard had walked to and fro, from one corner of the street to the other.

'Your wife . . .' protested Maigret.

'It doesn't matter.'

'Shouldn't you be at your dance hall?'

'What dance hall?'

Maigret stumbled noisily up the stairs to his apartment. Flinging open the door, he announced solemnly:

'Say hello to the newest inspector in the chief's squad.'

'Where's your hat?' Running his hand over his head, he realized he must have left his hat somewhere.

'That's women for you! And take note, be sure to take note, because it's very important . . . Very important, do you hear? . . . It's not because of the chief inspector . . . They had their eye on me, but I wasn't aware . . . Do you know what he said to me? . . . The big chief . . . He said . . . I can't repeat everything he said, but he's a father . . . He's a father to me, you know . . .'

Then she brought him his slippers and made a cup of strong coffee.

INSPECTOR MAIGRET

# OTHER TITLES IN THE SERIES

And more to follow